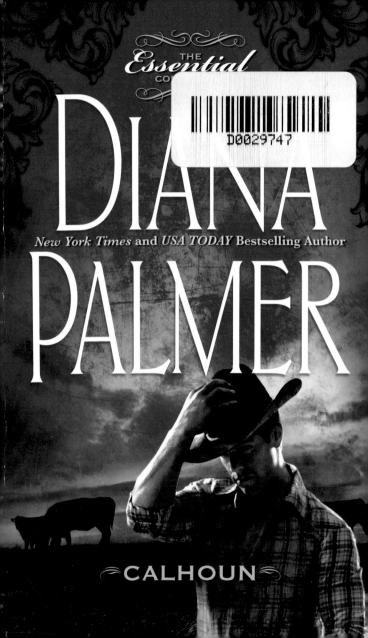

THE **Essential**
COLLECTION

DIANA

New York Times and *USA TODAY* Bestselling Author

PALMER

≈ CALHOUN ≈

ISBN-13:978-0-373-36364-3

EAN

Dear Reader,

I really can't express how flattered I am and also how grateful I am to Harlequin Books for releasing this collection of my published works. It came as a great surprise. I never think of myself as writing books that are collectible. In fact, there are days when I forget that writing is work at all. What I do for a living is so much fun that it never seems like a job. And since I reside in a small community, and my daily life is confined to such mundane things as feeding the wild birds and looking after my herb patch in the backyard, I feel rather unconnected from what many would think of as a glamorous profession.

But when I read my email, or when I get letters from readers, or when I go on signing trips to bookstores to meet all of you, I feel truly blessed. Over the past thirty years I have made lasting friendships with many of you. And quite frankly, most of you are like part of my family. You can't imagine how much you enrich my life. Thank you so much.

I also need to extend thanks to my family (my husband, James, son, Blayne, daughter-in-law, Christina, and granddaughter, Selena Marie), to my best friend, Ann, to my readers, booksellers and the wonderful people at Harlequin Books—from my editor of many years, Tara, to all the other fine and talented people who make up our publishing house. Thanks to all of you for making this job and my private life so worth living.

Thank you for this tribute, Harlequin, and for putting up with me for thirty long years! Love to all of you.

Diana Palmer

DIANA PALMER

The prolific author of more than a hundred books, Diana Palmer got her start as a newspaper reporter. A multi–*New York Times* bestselling author and one of the top ten romance writers in America, she has a gift for telling the most sensual tales with charm and humor. Diana lives with her family in Cornelia, Georgia.

Visit her website at www.DianaPalmer.com.

THE Essential COLLECTION

New York Times and *USA TODAY* Bestselling Author

DIANA PALMER

CALHOUN

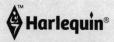

TORONTO NEW YORK LONDON
AMSTERDAM PARIS SYDNEY HAMBURG
STOCKHOLM ATHENS TOKYO MILAN MADRID
PRAGUE WARSAW BUDAPEST AUCKLAND

To Mary Wheeler at Micro Pro—thanks a million!

Recycling programs
for this product may
not exist in your area.

ISBN-13: 978-0-373-36364-3

CALHOUN

Printed in U.S.A.

New York Times and *USA TODAY*
Bestselling Author

Diana Palmer

The Essential Collection
Long, Tall Texans...and More!

Chapter 1

Abby couldn't help looking over her shoulder from time to time as she stood in line at the theater ticket counter. She'd escaped by telling Justin that she was going to see an art exhibit. Calhoun, thank God, was off somewhere buying more cattle, although he was certain to be home later this evening. When he found out where his ward had been, he'd be furious. She almost grinned at her own craftiness.

Well, it took craftiness to deal with Calhoun Ballenger. He and Justin, his older brother, had taken Abby in when she'd been just fifteen. They would have been her stepbrothers, except that an untimely car accident had killed their father and Abby's mother just two days before the couple were to have gotten married. There hadn't been any other family, so Calhoun had proposed that he and Justin assume responsibility for the heartbroken teenager, Abigail Clark. And they did.

It was legal, of course; technically Abby was Calhoun's ward. The problem was that she couldn't make Calhoun realize that she was a woman.

Abby sighed. That was a problem, all right. And to make it even worse, he'd gone crazy on the subject of protecting her from the world. For the past four months it had been a major ordeal just to go out on a date. The way he stood watch over her was getting almost comical. Justin rarely smiled, but Calhoun's antics brought him close to it.

Calhoun's attitude didn't amuse Abby, though. She was desperately in love with Calhoun, but the big blond man still looked upon her as a child. And despite her frequent attempts to show Calhoun that she was a woman, she couldn't seem to get through his armor.

She shifted restlessly. She had no idea of how to attract a man like Calhoun in the first place. He wasn't as much of a rounder now as he had been in his youth, but she knew that he was frequently seen in nightclubs in San Antonio with one sophisticated beauty or another. And here was Abby, dying of love for him. She wasn't sophisticated or beautiful. She was a rather plain country girl, not the sort to immediately draw men's eyes, even though her figure was better than average.

After brooding over the problem, she had come up with a solution. If she could manage to get sophisticated, he might notice her. Going to a strip show wasn't exactly the best first step, but in Jacobsville it was a good start. Just being seen here would show Calhoun that she wasn't the little prude he thought she was. *When* he found out about it—and eventually he would hear she'd attended the show.

Abby smoothed the waistline of her pretty gray plaid skirt. She was wearing a pale yellow blouse with it, and her long, wavy brown hair was in a neat chignon. Her hair, when it was loose, was one of her best assets. It was thick and silky. And her eyes weren't bad. They were big, quiet grayish-blue eyes, and she was blessed with a peaches-and-cream complexion and a perfect bow of a mouth. But without careful makeup she was hopelessly plain. Her breasts were bigger than she wanted them to be, her legs longer than she would have liked. She had friends who were small and dainty, and they made her feel like a beanpole. She glanced down at herself miserably. If only she were petite and exquisitely beautiful.

At least she did look older and more sophisticated than usual in her burgundy velour jacket, and her blue-gray eyes sparkled as she thought about what she was doing. Well, it wasn't so bad for a woman to go to a male dance revue, was it? She had to get educated somehow, and God knew Calhoun wasn't about to let her date any men who knew the score. He saw to it that her only escorts were boys her own age, and he screened every one and made casual remarks about how often he cleaned his guns and what he thought about "fooling around before marriage." It wasn't really surprising to Abby that few of her dates came back.

She shivered a little in the cold night air. It was February, and cold even in south Texas. As she huddled in her jacket, she smiled at another young woman shivering in the long line outside the Grand Theater. It was the only theater in Jacobsville, and there had been some opposition to having this kind of entertainment come to town. But in the end there had been surprisingly few complaints, and there was a long line of women waiting to see if these men lived up to the publicity.

Wouldn't Calhoun just die when he found out what

she'd done? She grinned. His blond-streaked brown hair would stand on end, and his dark eyes would glare at her furiously. Justin would do what he always did—he'd go out and dig postholes while Calhoun wound down. The two brothers looked a lot alike, except that Justin's hair was almost black. They both had dark eyes, and they were both tall, muscular men. Calhoun was by far the handsomer of the two. Justin had a craggy face and a reticent personality, and although he was courteous to women, he never dated anybody. Almost everybody knew why—Shelby Jacobs had thrown him over years ago, refusing to marry him.

That had been when the Ballengers had still been poor, before Justin's business sense and Calhoun's feel for marketing had skyrocketed them to success with a mammoth feedlot operation here in south Texas. Shelby's family was rich, and rumor had it that she thought Justin was beneath her. It had certainly made him bitter. Funny, she mused, Shelby seemed like such a wonderful woman. And her brother, Tyler, was nice, too.

Two more ladies got their tickets, and Abby dug out a ten-dollar bill. Just as she got to the ticket counter, though, her wrist was suddenly seized and she was pulled unceremoniously to one side.

"I thought I recognized that jacket," Calhoun murmured, glaring down at her with eyes that were dark and faintly glittering. "What a good thing I decided to come home through town. Where's my brother?" he added for good measure. "Does he know where you are?"

"I told him I was going to an art exhibit," Abby replied with a touch of her irrepressible humor. Her blue-gray eyes twinkled up at him, and she felt the warm glow she always felt when Calhoun came close. Even when he was angry, it was so good to be near him. "Well, it is an art exhibit, sort of," she argued when he looked skeptical. "Except that the male statues are alive…"

"My God." He stared at the line of amused women and abruptly turned toward his white Jaguar, tugging at her wrist. "Let's go."

"I'm not going home," she said firmly, struggling. It was exciting to challenge him. "I'm going to buy my ticket and go in there—Calhoun!" she wailed as he ended the argument by simply lifting her in his hard arms and carrying her to the car.

"I can't even leave the state for one day without you doing something insane," Calhoun muttered in his deep, gravelly voice. "The last time I went off on business, I came home to find you about to leave for Lake Tahoe with that Misty Davies."

"Congratulations. You saved me from a weekend of skiing," Abby murmured dryly. Not for the world would she have admitted how exciting it was to have him carry her, to feel his strength at such close quarters. He was as strong as he looked, and the subtle scents of his body and the warmth of his breath on her face made her body tingle in new and exciting ways.

"There were two college boys all set to go along, as I remember," he reminded her.

"What am I supposed to do with my car?" she demanded. "Leave it here?"

"Why not? God knows nobody would be stupid enough to steal it," he replied easily, and kept walking, her slight weight soft and disturbing in his hard arms.

"It's a very nice little car," she protested, talking more than usual because the feel of his chest was unnerving her. His clean-shaven chin was just above her, and she was getting drunk on the feel of him.

"Which you wouldn't have if I'd gone with you instead of Justin," he returned. "Honest to God, he spoils you rotten. He should have married Shelby and had kids of his own to ruin. I hate having him practice on you. That damned little sports car isn't safe."

"It's mine, I like it, I'm making the payments and I'm keeping it," she said shortly.

He looked down at her, his dark eyes much too close to hers. "Aren't we brave, though?" he taunted softly, deliberately letting his gaze fall on her mouth.

She could barely breathe, but he wasn't going to make her back down. Not that way. She didn't dare let him see the effect he had on her. "I'm almost twenty-one," she reminded him. He looked into her eyes, and she felt the impact of his glance like a body blow. It made her feel like a lead weight. And there was a sudden tautness about his body that puzzled her. For seconds that strung out like hours, he searched her eyes. Then abruptly he moved again.

"So you keep telling me," he replied curtly. "And then you go and do something stupid like this."

"There's nothing wrong with being sophisticated," she mumbled. "God knows how I'll ever get an education. You seem to want me to spend the rest of my life a virgin."

"Hang out in this kind of atmosphere and you won't stay in that sainted condition for much longer," he returned angrily. She disturbed him when she made such statements. She had been talking like that for months, and he was no nearer a solution to the problem than he had been at the beginning. He quickened his pace toward the car, his booted feet making loud, angry thuds on the pavement.

Calhoun was still wearing a dark suit, Abby noticed. His thick dark-blond hair was covered by his cream dress Stetson. He smelled of Oriental cologne, and his dark face was clean-shaven. He was a handsome brute, Abby thought. Sexy and overpoweringly masculine, and she loved every line of him, every scowl, every rugged inch. She forced her screaming nerves not to give her away and attempted to hide her attraction to him, as usual, with humor.

"Aren't we in a temper, though?" she taunted softly, and his dark expression hardened. It was exciting to make him mad. She'd only realized that in the past few weeks, but more and more she liked to prod him, to see his explosive reactions. She loved the touch of his hands, and provoking him had become addictive. "I'm a big girl. I graduated from the trade school last year. I have a diploma. I'm a secretary. I'm working for Mr. Bundy at the feedlot sales office—"

"I remember. I paid for the trade school courses and got you the damned job," he said tersely.

"You sure did, Calhoun," she agreed, her mischievous gaze darting up at him as he opened the passenger door of the vehicle and put her on the smooth leather seat, slamming the door once she was settled. He went around the gleaming hood and got in under the steering wheel. There was muted violence in the way he started the powerful white car, shot away from the curb and drove down the main town's street.

"Abby, I can't believe you really wanted to pay money to watch a bunch of boys take their clothes off," he muttered.

"It beats having boys try to take mine off," she

returned humorously. "You must think so, too, because you go nuts if I try to date anybody with any experience."

He frowned. That was true. It upset him to think of any man taking advantage of Abby. He didn't want other men touching her.

"I'd beat a man to his knees for trying to undress you, and that's a fact," he said.

"My poor future husband," she sighed. "I can see him now, calling the police on our wedding night…"

"You're years too young to talk about getting married," he said.

"I'll be twenty-one in three months. My mother was twenty-one when she had me," she reminded him.

"I'm thirty-two, and I've never been married," he replied. "There's plenty of time. You don't need to rush into marriage before you've had time to see something of the world," he said firmly.

"How can I?" she asked reasonably. "You won't let me."

He glared at her. "It's the part of life that you're trying to see that bothers me. Male strip shows. My God."

"They weren't going to take all their clothes off," she assured him. "Just most of them."

"Why did you decide to go tonight?"

"I didn't have anything else to do," she sighed. "And Misty had been to see this show."

"Misty Davies," he muttered. "I've told you I don't approve of your friendship with that flighty heiress. She's years older than you and much more sophisticated."

"No wonder," she replied. "She doesn't have an overbearing guardian who's determined to save her from herself."

"She could have used one. A woman who treats her body cheaply doesn't invite a wedding ring."

"So you keep saying. At least Misty won't faint of shock on her wedding night when her husband takes his clothes off. I've never seen a man without a stitch on. Except in this magazine that Misty had—" she began, warming to her subject.

"For God's sake, you shouldn't be reading that kind of magazine!" He looked outraged.

Her eyebrows went up suddenly, and her eyes were as round as saucers. "Why not?"

He searched for words. "Well…because!"

"Men ogle women in those kind of magazines," she said reasonably. "If we can be exploited, why can't men?"

He finally gave in to ill temper. "Why can't you just shut up, Abby?"

"Okay, Calhoun, I'll do that very thing," she agreed. She studied his hard, angry profile, and almost smiled at the way she'd gotten him ruffled. He might not be in love with her, but she certainly did have a knack for getting his attention.

"All this sudden fascination with male nudity," he grumbled, glaring at her. "I don't know what's gotten into you."

"Frustration," she replied. "It comes from too many nights sitting home alone."

"I've never tried to stop you from dating," he said defensively.

"Oh, no, of course you haven't. You just sit with my prospective dates and make a big deal of cleaning your gun collection while you air your archaic views on premarital sex!"

"They're not archaic," he said curtly. "A lot of men feel the way I do about it."

"Do tell?" She lifted her eyebrow. "And I suppose that means that you're a virgin, too, Calhoun?"

His dark eyes cut sideways at her. "Do you think so, Abby?" he asked, in a tone she'd never heard him use.

She suddenly felt very young. The huskiness in his deep voice, added to the faint arrogance in his dark eyes, made her feel foolish for even having asked. Of course he wasn't a virgin.

She averted her eyes. "Foolish question," she murmured softly.

"Wasn't it, though?" He pressed on the accelerator. For some reason, it bothered him to have Abby know what his private life was like. She probably knew more than he'd given her credit for, especially if she was hanging around with Misty Davies. Misty frequented the same kind of city hot spots that Calhoun did, and she'd seen him with one or two of his occasional companions. He hoped Misty hadn't talked to Abby about what she'd seen, but he couldn't count on it.

His sudden withdrawal puzzled Abby. She didn't like the cold silence that was growing between them any more than she liked thinking about his women. "How did you know where I was?" she asked to break the rigid silence.

"I didn't, honey," he confessed. The endearment sounded so natural coming from him that she'd never minded him using it, though she disliked its artificiality when other men did. "I happened to come home through Jacobsville. And who should I see in line—in front of all the lurid posters—but you?"

She sighed. "Fate. Fate is out to get me."

"Fate may not be the only one," he returned, but his voice was so low that she couldn't hear.

He turned onto the road that led past the feedlot to the big Spanish house where the Ballengers lived. On the way they passed the Jacobs's colonial-style house, far off the road at the end of a paved driveway, with purebred Arabian horses grazing in sprawling pastures dotted with oak trees. There wasn't much grass—the weather was still cold, and a few snow flurries had caused excitement the day before. Big bales of hay were placed around the property to give the horses adequate feed, supplemented with blocks of vitamins and minerals.

"I hear the Jacobses are having financial problems," Abby remarked absently.

He glanced at her. "Since the old man died last summer, they're close to bankrupt, in fact Tyler's borrowed all he can borrow. If he can't pull it together now, he never will. The old man made deals Ty didn't even know about. If he loses that place, it's going to be damned hard on his pride."

"Hard on Shelby's, too," she remarked.

He grimaced. "For God's sake, don't mention Shelby around Justin."

"I wouldn't dare. He gets funny, doesn't he?"

"I wouldn't call throwing punches at people funny."

"I've seen you throw punches a time or two," she reminded him, recalling one particular day not too long before when one of the new cowhands had beaten a horse. Calhoun had knocked the man to his knees and fired him on the spot, his voice so cold and quiet that it had cut to the bone. Calhoun didn't have to raise his voice. Like Justin, when Calhoun lost his temper he had a look that made words unnecessary.

He was an odd mixture, she thought, studying him. So tenderhearted that he'd go off for half a day by himself if he had to put down a calf or if something happened to one of his men. And so hotheaded at times that the men would actually hide from his anger. In temperament, he was like Justin. They were both strong, fiery men, but underneath there was a tenderness, a vulnerability, that very few people ever saw. Abby, because she'd lived with them for so many years, knew them better than any outsider ever could.

"How did you get back so fast?" she asked to break the silence.

He shrugged. "I guess I've got radar," he murmured, smiling faintly. "I had a feeling you wouldn't be sitting at home with Justin watching old war movies on the VCR."

"I didn't think you'd be back before morning."

"So you decided you'd go watch a lot of muscle men strip off and wiggle on the stage."

"Heaven knows I tried." She sighed theatrically. "Now I'll die ignorant, thanks to you."

"Damn it all," he laughed, taken aback by her reactions. She made him laugh more than any woman he'd ever known. And lately he'd found himself thinking about her more than he should. Maybe it was just his age, he thought. He'd been alone a long time, and a woman here and there didn't really satisfy him. But Abby wasn't fair game. She was a marrying girl, and he'd better remember that. No way could he seduce her for pleasure, so he had to keep the fires banked down. If he could.

Justin was in his study when they got back, frowning darkly over some figures in his books. When he looked up, his craggy face was devoid of expression, but his dark eyes twinkled when he glanced from Calhoun's irritated expression to Abby's furious one.

"How was the art show?" he asked her.

"It wasn't an art show," Calhoun said flatly, tossing his Stetson onto the coffee table. "It was a male strip show."

Justin's pencil stopped in midair as he stared at Abby. His shock was a little embarrassing, because Justin was even more old-fashioned and reactionary than Calhoun about such things. He wouldn't even talk about anything intimate in mixed company.

"A what?" Justin asked.

"A male revue," Abby countered, glaring at Calhoun. "It's a kind of…variety show."

"Hell," Calhoun retorted, his dark eyes flashing. "It's a strip show!"

"Abby!" Justin scolded.

"I'm almost twenty-one," she told him. "I have a responsible job. I drive a car. I'm old enough to marry and have children. If I want to go and see a male variety show—" she ignored Calhoun's instantly inserted "strip show" "—I have every right."

Justin laid his pencil down and lit a cigarette. Calhoun glared at him, and so did Abby, but he ignored them. The only concession he made to their disapproval was to turn on one of the eight smokeless ashtrays they'd bought him for Christmas.

"That sounds like a declaration of war," Justin remarked.

Abby lifted her chin. "That's what it is." She turned to Calhoun. "If you don't stop embarrassing me in front of the whole world, I'll move in with Misty Davies."

Calhoun's good intentions went up in smoke. "Like

hell you will," he countered. "You're not living with that woman!"

"I'll live with her if I want to!"

"If you two would..." Justin began calmly.

"Over my dead body!" Calhoun raged, moving closer. "She has parties that last for days!"

"...just try to communicate..." Justin continued.

"She likes people! She's a socialite!" Abby's eyes were almost black now as she clenched her fists by her side and glared up at Calhoun.

"...you just might..." Justin went on.

"She's a featherbrained, overstimulated eccentric!" Calhoun retorted.

"*...COME TO AN UNDERSTANDING!*" Justin thundered, rising out of his chair with blazing eyes.

They both froze at the unfamiliar sound of his raised voice. He never shouted, not even when he was at his angriest.

"Damn, I hurt my ears," Justin sighed, putting his palm to one while he glared at his brother and Abby. "Now, listen, this isn't getting you anywhere. Besides that, any minute Maria and Lopez are going to come running in here thinking someone's been murdered." Just as he finished speaking, two robed, worried elderly people appeared, wide-eyed and apprehensive, in the doorway. "Now see what you've done," Justin grumbled.

"What is all this noise about?" Maria asked, pushing back her long salt-and-pepper hair and glancing worriedly around the room. "We thought something terrible had happened."

"*¡Ay de mí!* Another rumble." Lopez shook his head and grinned at Abby. "What have you done now, *niñita?*"

She glared at him. "Nothing," she said tersely. "Not one thing—"

"She went to a male strip show," Calhoun volunteered.

"I did not!" she protested, red faced.

"What is the world coming to?" Maria shook her head, put her hands to it and went out mumbling in Spanish, followed by a chuckling Lopez. The couple, married more than thirty years, had been with the family for two generations. They were family, not just cook and former horse wrangler.

"But, I didn't!" Abby called after them. She darted a speaking glance at Calhoun, who was perched on a corner of Justin's desk looking elegant and imperturbable. "Now see what you've done!"

"Me?" Calhoun asked coolly. "Hell, you're the one with the lurid curiosity."

"Lurid?" She gaped at him. "Go ahead, tell me you've never been to a female strip show."

Calhoun got up, looking uncomfortable. "That's different."

"Oh, sure it is. Women are sex objects but men aren't, right?"

"She's got you there," Justin said.

Calhoun glared at both of them, turned on his heel and left the room. Abby gazed after him smugly, feeling as if she'd won at least a minor victory. There was little consolation in her triumph, though. Calhoun had been harder to get along with than a bone-dry snake at a poison water hole lately. She didn't know how or what, but she was going to have to do something about the situation, and soon.

Chapter 2

Abby arranged to miss breakfast the next morning. Calhoun's attitude irritated her. He didn't want her himself, but he was so possessive that she couldn't get near another man. His attitude was frustrating at best. He had no idea how she felt, of course. She was careful to hide her feelings for him. A man like Calhoun, who was rich and moderately handsome, could have any woman he wanted. He wouldn't want a plain, unsophisticated woman like Abby. She knew that, and it hurt. It made her rebellious, too. She didn't want to spend the rest of her life grieving for a man she could never have. It was far better to look in other directions. But how could she, when Calhoun refused to let go?

She drove several miles from the ranch to the office at the mammoth feedlot in the small red British sports car she'd talked Justin into cosigning for when she'd graduated from the local vocational school. Because of the attention Calhoun and Justin paid to hygiene, there wasn't as much odor as most feedlots generated, which surprised a lot of visiting cattlemen. Abby had once gone with Calhoun to tour some other feedlots and had come out with a new respect for the one back home. The Ballenger brothers' operation was a little more expensive to run, but there were hardly any cattle deaths here because of disease. And that was a prime consideration. A rancher who contracted with the feedlot to fatten his cattle for slaughter didn't want to lose the animals to disease.

Since Abby was early, the office was deserted. There were three other women who worked here, all married, and they helped keep records on the various herds of feeder cattle being fattened for ranches all over the country. There were contracts to sort and file, records on each lot of cattle to keep, and ongoing vaccination and management reports. There was the constant hum of the heavy equipment used to feed the cattle and to remove waste to underground storage to be used later to fertilize pastures where grain was grown. The phones rang constantly and the computers had to be programmed. There was a payroll department, as well as a salesman, a staff veterinarian and a number of cowboys who moved cattle in and out and saw to feeding them and maintaining the machinery that kept it all going. Abby hadn't realized until she'd come to work here how big the operation was.

The sheer size of it was staggering, even for Texas. Fenced areas filled with steers stretched to the horizon, and the dust was formidable, as was the smell, which was inevitable even when sanitary management practices were employed.

The Ballengers didn't own a packing plant—that

wasn't legal, just as it wasn't legal for packers to own custom feedlots. But the brothers did own a third of their feeder cattle, and the other two-thirds were custom fed. Abby had grown up hearing terms like profit margin, break-even prices and ration formulation. Now she understood what the words meant.

She put her purse under her desk and turned on her computer. There were several new contracts waiting to be filled in for new lots of four-footed customers.

The feedlot took in feeder cattle weighing six hundred to seven hundred pounds and fed them up to their slaughter weight of one thousand to eleven hundred pounds. The Ballengers had a resident nutritionist and an experienced stockman who handled the twice-daily feeding routine with its highly automated machinery. They had the feeding down to such a fine art that the Ballenger operation was included in the top five percent of feedlots nationally. And that was a real honor, considering all the things that could go wrong, from falling cattle prices to unexpected epidemics to drought.

Abby was fascinated by the workings of it all. There were thousands of bawling steers and heifers out there. There were always big cattle trucks coming and going and men yelling and herding and vaccinating and dehorning, and the noise could get deafening despite the soundproofed office walls. Visiting cattlemen came to see their investments. Those who didn't come were sent monthly progress reports. Daily records were kept on everything.

Abby fed the first contract into her electronic typewriter, trying to decipher the spidery scrawl of Caudell Ayker, the feedlot office manager. He was second only to Calhoun in the chain of command, because Calhoun's name went in as manager. He and Justin owned the feedlot jointly, but Justin held the lion's share of the stock. Justin preferred money management to meeting with clients, so Calhoun did most of the day-to-day management on the feedlot. That was one reason Abby loved the job. It meant she got to see a lot of Calhoun.

When Calhoun walked in the door in a dashing pale tan suit, Abby hit the wrong key, covering the contract with a flock of *X*s. She grimaced, backspacing to correct her mistake, and then discovered that she couldn't do it. The correction was too little, too late. Irritated, she ripped the paper out of the machine, put a clean sheet in and started all over again.

"Having problems this morning, honey?" Calhoun asked with his usual cheerful smile, despite the way they'd parted in anger the night before. He never carried grudges. It was one of his virtues.

"Just the usual frustrations, boss," she answered with a blithe smile.

He searched her eyes. They had such a peculiar light in them lately. He found her more and more disturbing, especially when she wore close-fitting suits like the blue one she had on today. It clung lovingly to every line of her tall, slender body, outlining the thrust of her high breasts, the smooth curve of her hips. He took a slow breath, trying to hide his growing attraction to her. It was odd how she'd managed to get under his skin so easily.

"You look nice," he said unexpectedly.

She felt color blush her cheeks, and she smiled. "Thank you."

He hesitated without knowing why, his dark eyes

caressing her face, her mouth. "I don't like your hair like that," he added quietly. "I like it long and loose."

She was having a hard time breathing. Her eyes worked up his broad chest to his face and were trapped by his steady gaze. Like electricity, something burst between them, linking them, until she had to drag her eyes down again. Her legs actually trembled.

"I'd better get back to work," she said unsteadily, fiddling with the paper.

"We both had," he replied. He turned and walked into his office without knowing how he got there. Once inside, he sat down behind his big oak desk and stared through the open door at Abby until the buzz of the intercom reminded him of the day's business.

Things went smoothly for a little while, but it was too much to expect that the serenity would last. Just before lunch, one of the cattlemen who had feeder steers in the lot came by to check on them and got an eyeful of Abby.

"You sure are a pretty little thing," the man said, grinning down at the picture she made in her neat blue knit suit and white blouse with her hair in a French twist and a minimum of makeup on her pretty face. He was about Calhoun's age.

She flushed. The man wasn't as handsome as Calhoun, but he was pleasant-looking and he seemed harmless. "Thank you," she said demurely, and smiled at him, just as she smiled at other customers. But he took it as an invitation.

He sat down on the corner of her desk, giving her a purely masculine scrutiny with his pale blue eyes. "I'm Greg Myers," he introduced himself. "I just stopped in on my way to Oklahoma City, and I thought I'd take Calhoun to lunch if he's in. But I think I'd rather take you instead." He lowered his voice, then reached out unexpectedly and touched Abby's cheek, ignoring her indrawn breath. "You pretty little thing. You look like a tea rose, ripe for the picking."

Abby just gaped at him. All her reading and imagining hadn't prepared her for this kind of flirtation with an experienced man. She was out of her depth and frankly stunned.

"Come on, now," Myers drawled, caressing her cheek. "Say you will. We'll have a nice long lunch and get to know each other."

While Abby was searching for the right words to extricate herself from the unwelcome situation, Calhoun came out of his office and stood directly behind Mr. Myers, looking suddenly murderous.

"I'm afraid you'll have to settle for me," Calhoun said tersely. "Abby's my ward, and she doesn't date older men."

"Oops." Myers stood up, grinning sheepishly. "Sorry, old son, I didn't know."

"No harm done," Calhoun said carelessly, but his eyes were dark and cold and dangerous-looking. "Let's go. Abby, I'll want the latest progress report on his cattle when we get back."

Only a few months before, Abby might have had some snappy reply to that, or she might have jumped back at Calhoun for acting so possessive. But now she just looked at him, feeling helpless and hungry and awash on a wave of longing because he was acting jealous.

He seemed to stop breathing, too. His dark eyes searched hers, aware of her embarrassment, her confusion. He let his gaze fall to her mouth and watched her lips part suddenly, and his body reacted in a way that shocked him.

"Lunch. Now." Calhoun ushered the other cattleman to the door. "If you'll get in the car, I'll just get my hat and be right with you," he told the man with a glued-on smile and a pat on the shoulder. "That's right, you go ahead…." He turned to Abby, his expression unreadable. "I want to talk to you." Calhoun took her arm and pulled her up, leading her into his office without a word. He closed the door, and the way he looked at her made her feel threatened and wildly excited all at the same time.

"Mr. Myers is waiting…." she faltered, disturbed by the darkness of his eyes as they met hers.

He moved toward her, and she backed up until his desk stopped her, her eyes riveted to his. Maybe he was going to make a declaration!

His chin lifted then, and it was anger that glinted in his dark eyes, not possessiveness. "Listen," he said curtly, "Grey Myers has had three wives. He currently has at least one mistress. He's forgotten more than you've had time to learn. I don't want you to learn that kind of lesson with a professional Romeo."

"I'm going to learn it with someone eventually," she said, swallowing hard. Her body felt odd, taut and tingling all at once, because his was close enough that she could feel its warm strength.

"I know that," he said impatiently, and his face hardened. "But I'd just as soon you didn't join a queue. Myers is no serious suitor. He's a playboy with a smooth manner, and he'd have you screaming for help five minutes after you were alone with him."

So that was it. More big-brother responsibility. He wasn't jealous, he was upset because his protective instincts had been aroused. She stared at the steady rise and fall of his chest in dull acceptance. *Stupid me,* she thought miserably, *wishing for a star again.*

"I wasn't trying to lead him on," she said finally. "I just smiled at him, like I smile at everyone—even you. I guess he thought I was sending out smoke signals, but I wasn't, honestly."

His face relaxed. "No harm done." And then he moved. One long, powerful arm slid behind her, bringing his lips within an inch of hers. She almost moaned at the minty warmth of his breath on her mouth. Her gaze dropped to his mouth, curiously tracing every hard line of the thin upper lip and the more chiseled lower one. Her heart throbbed. Her breath seemed to stop altogether, and for one long instant she felt the full weight of his chest against her soft breasts in a contact that was shocking. She looked up at him with wide, stunned eyes.

Then he moved back, the hat he'd been reaching for in one hand, his eyes frankly amused at the look on her face. So she'd never thought of him that way, had she? It irritated him to think that she didn't feel the new and very unwelcome attraction he was discovering for her. It was just as well that he had a business function tonight; it would keep his overimaginative brain away from Abby.

"Were you expecting something?" he asked coldly. "I just wanted my hat." He watched a shadow pass across her eyes before she mumbled something and lowered her gaze. He put his Stetson on his thick blond-streaked hair and tilted it over one eye. "I hired you to work here, not to send out signals, intentional or otherwise, to clients."

"I hate you," she said suddenly, sick of his accusations and his hateful remarks.

"Sure you do. What else is new?" He tapped her chin with a long finger. "Get busy."

While she was still struggling with her composure he opened the door and went out without a backward glance.

Abby hardly got anything done for the next hour. She couldn't remember a time when she'd felt so turned around, so confused. She was sure she hated Calhoun, but in an hour he'd be back, smiling, and then she'd forgive him. That was what made her so miserable, the knowledge that he could commit murder and she'd still love him. Damn this hateful attraction!

She took a half-hour break and went to the canteen and had a sandwich that she didn't taste. She was barely back at her desk when Mr. Myers returned—with Justin instead of Calhoun.

She handed the progress reports to Justin, who herded Mr. Myers into his brother's office, kept him there a scant ten minutes and then herded him out again. Abby kept her head down and didn't even say hello. That was just as well, because Mr. Myers didn't look in her direction.

Justin gave Abby a curious look afterward. "That's unusual," he remarked. "Calhoun called me out of a board meeting to have lunch and talk over that contract with Myers. Then he waltzed off and left me there. What's going on?"

Abby cleared her throat. "Why, Justin, I have no idea," she said, even managing a smile. Justin lifted an eyebrow, shrugged and went back into Calhoun's office without another word. Abby stared after him, curious herself about Calhoun's behavior. Then it occurred to her that maybe he just didn't like Greg Myers, which led to the unpalatable thought that perhaps they'd fallen out over a woman. Maybe one of Myers's mistresses… She turned back to her typewriter. She hated even thinking about that side of Calhoun's life.

Justin was quiet for the rest of the afternoon, but he had plenty to say when Calhoun came in just before quitting time. The door was half-open, and Abby, who was the last of the office group to leave, got an earful as she was straightening up her desk.

"This has got to stop," Justin was telling his brother. "One of the office girls told me that Myers got friendly with Abby just before you cleared out. It's gotten to the point that Abby can't even smile at a man without having you come down on her head like Judgment. She's almost twenty-one. It isn't fair to expect her to live like a recluse."

"I wasn't," Calhoun said curtly. "I just warned her off him. My God, you know his reputation!"

"Abby's no fool," came the reply. "She's a levelheaded person."

"Sure, she's proved that," Calhoun said with biting sarcasm. "Going to a strip show—"

"It was not!" Abby called through the open door. "It was a male variety show."

"My God, she's standing out there listening!" Calhoun jerked the door all the way open, glaring at her. "Stop eavesdropping! It isn't polite!"

"Stop talking about me behind my back, then," she returned, picking up her purse. "I wouldn't have gone out with a man like Grey Myers even to spite you, Calhoun. I know a line when I hear one."

Calhoun glared at her. "I'm not sure it's a good idea, your working here."

Her eyebrows went up. "Really? Why?"

"The place is full of men," Calhoun muttered, and Justin had to smother a grin.

Abby lifted her eyebrows and smiled. "Why, so it is," she gushed. "Lovely, unshaven men who smell of cattle and cow chips. Sooo romantic," she sighed.

Justin had turned away. Calhoun's dark eyes were glittering.

"Myers didn't smell of cow chips," he reminded her.

She arched her eyebrows at him. "How interesting that you noticed," she said in a theatrical whisper.

He looked as if he wanted to throw something at her. "Will you cut that out?" he muttered.

She sighed. "Suit yourself. I was just trying to help. God forbid that I should be seduced by some strange, sweet-smelling man."

"Go home!" Calhoun roared.

"My, my, what a nasty temper we're in," she said demurely. She reached for her purse, glancing back at him. "I'll have Maria make you a nice bowl of razor-blade soup, just to keep your tongue sharp."

"I won't be home for supper, thank God," Calhoun said coldly. "I've got a date," he added, for no other reason than to irritate her. He didn't like the idea of her knowing how much Myers's flirting had upset him. He didn't want her to know that he'd been so violently jealous that he couldn't even trust himself to have lunch with the man and had had to call Justin to intervene.

But Abby didn't know that, and she was sure that it was just Calhoun being overprotective as usual. It hurt her to hear about where he was going. Abby felt as if she were being choked to death. If only she were beautiful and blond, if only she could cope! But she managed to hide her emptiness. "That's great, Calhoun, you just enjoy yourself while I sit home alone. I'll never get a date as long as you're two steps behind me."

"Dream on," Calhoun told her. "Hell will freeze over before you'd go out with a man like that."

"There's a little town called Hell, you know," Abby told him. "It does snow there…."

"If I were you I'd go home, Abby," Justin said, eyeing his brother. "It's Friday night. You might find a nice movie to watch. Come to think of it, I just bought a new war movie. You can watch it with me if you want to."

She smiled. Justin really was nice. "Thanks. I might do that, since my watchdog doesn't want me out after dark," she added with a glare at Calhoun. "I'll bet Elizabeth the First had a guardian just like you!"

Justin caught Calhoun in the nick of time, and Abby took off running, her heart in her throat. It was odd how Calhoun, usually so easygoing, had turned explosive lately. She did goad him, of course, but she couldn't help it. Fighting him was the only way she could stay sane and hide her feelings for him. If she ever started batting her eyelashes and sighing over him, he'd probably shoot her off the place like a bullet.

She started her car and drove home, all the fury dying into misery as she left the feedlot behind. What good was pretending? Her heart was broken, because Calhoun was going out with one of his women and she didn't qualify for that title. She never would. She'd grow old with Calhoun patting her on the head. Once or twice she'd almost thought he felt something for her, that he'd begun to notice her. But if he had, he certainly wouldn't be running all over the place with other women. And he wouldn't ignore Abby unless she started a fight or got into trouble. She was his responsibility, of course. His headache. To him she was anything but a warm, attractive woman whom he might love eventually. That she'd never be.

By the time she got to the house, she felt sick all over, but a plan was beginning to form in her mind. If Calhoun thought she was giving in that easily, he was in for a shock. She could have a good time, too, even if she didn't have a date. By golly, she'd get out and find herself one!

Chapter 3

Abby ate a solitary meal. Justin was called to the phone shortly after they got home, and he told Maria to put his dinner on a tray so he could eat it while he watched the movie he'd bought. Calhoun had come home to change for his date, and Abby had made a beeline for her room and stayed there until after he'd left. She didn't even care how it looked; she was sick at the thought of Calhoun with some faceless blonde. That was when she knew she had to break out, even if just for the evening.

She hadn't started out to rebel. But she couldn't sit home and watch the movie with Justin. She'd never hear a word of it; she'd just brood about Calhoun.

So she got dressed in slacks and a blouse and brushed her hair. Then she called Misty.

"How do you feel about helping me rebel?" she asked the older girl.

Misty laughed huskily. "You're lucky my date canceled out. Okay. I'm game. What are we rebelling against?"

"Calhoun caught me at the revue last night and dragged me home," Abby told her. "And today he... Well, never mind, but he set me off again. So tonight I thought I'd like to sample that new dance bar in Jacobsville."

"Now that is an idea worthy of you, Abby. I'll pick you up in fifteen minutes."

"I'll be ready."

Abby ran downstairs, giving no thought at all to how Calhoun was going to react to this latest rebellion. Well, he had his woman, damn him. Horrible pictures of his bronzed body in bed with the faceless blonde danced in front of Abby's eyes. No, she told herself, she wasn't going to let Calhoun's actions hurt her like that. She was going to get out and live!

She poked her head into the living room. Cigarette smoke drifted in front of a screen on which men in uniforms were blowing each other up.

"I'm going out with Misty," she told Justin.

He glanced up from where he was sitting. His long legs were crossed over the coffee table, and he had a snifter of brandy in one hand and a cigarette in the other. "Okay, honey," he said agreeably. "Stay out of trouble, will you? You and Calhoun are hell on the digestion lately, and he doesn't seem to need much excuse to go for your throat."

"I'll behave. Misty and I are just going to that new dance place. I'll be good, honest I will. Good night."

"Good night."

He went back to the bullets and bombs, and she closed the door with a sigh. Justin was so nice. He never tried to hog-tie her. Now why couldn't Calhoun be like that? She felt murderous when she considered Calhoun's possessiveness. She was entitled to a life that didn't revolve around him. There was just no sense in wearing her heart out on his taciturn indifference. None at all!

Misty came ten minutes later. Thank God, Calhoun didn't reappear. With a sigh of relief, Abby ran out to Misty's little sports car, all smiles, her breaking heart carefully concealed from her all-too-perceptive girlfriend.

It was Friday night, and the Jacobsville Dance Palace was booming. It had a live Western band on the weekends, and while it did serve hard liquor, it wasn't the kind of dive Calhoun had forbidden her to frequent. Not that she cared one whit about his strictures, of course.

Abby glanced apprehensively toward the doorway, across the crowded room where cigar and cigarette smoke made a gray haze under bright lights. The band's rhythm shook the rafters. Couples danced on the bare wood floor, the men in Western gear, the women in jeans and boots.

"Calhoun won't know you're here, I tell you." Misty laughed softly. "Honestly, it's ridiculous the way he dogs your footsteps lately."

"That's what I keep telling him, but it does no good at all," Abby replied miserably. "I just want to get out on my own."

"I'm doing my best," Misty assured her. "Any day now I'll have some new apartment prospects for us to look at. I've got a real estate agent helping."

"Good." Abby sipped her drink, trying not to notice the blatant stare she was getting from the man at the next table. He'd been eyeing her ever since she and Misty had walked in, and he was giving her the willies. He looked about Calhoun's age, but he lacked Calhoun's attractive masculinity. This man was dark headed and had a beer belly. He wasn't much taller than Abby, but what he lacked in height he made up in girth. He had a cowboy hat pulled low over his small eyes, and he was obviously intoxicated.

"He's staring at me again," Abby muttered. She lifted her gin and tonic to her lips, wondering at how much better it tasted every time she took a sip. She hated gin, but Misty had convinced her that she couldn't sit at the table drinking ginger ale.

"Don't worry," Misty patted her arm. "He'll give up and go away. There's Tyler! Hi, Ty!"

Tyler Jacobs was tall and rangy-looking. He had green eyes and an arrogant smile, and Abby was a little afraid of him. But he didn't carry his wealth around on his shoulders as some rich men did, and he wasn't a snob, even though the town of Jacobsville took its name from his grandfather.

"Hello, Misty. Abby." Tyler pulled out a chair and straddled it. "What are you doing here? Does Calhoun know?" he asked quietly.

Abby shifted restlessly in the chair and raised her glass to her lips again. "I am perfectly capable of drinking a drink if I want to," she said, enunciating carefully because her tongue suddenly felt thick. "And Calhoun doesn't own me."

"Oh, my God," Tyler sighed. He gave Misty a rueful glance. "Your doing, I gather?"

Misty blinked her long false lashes at Tyler, and her blue eyes twinkled. "I provided transportation, that's all. Abby is my friend. I'm helping her to rebel."

"You'll help get her killed if you aren't careful. Where's Calhoun?" he asked Abby.

"Out with one of his harem," she said with a mocking smile. "Not that I mind, as long as he's out of my hair for the evening," she added carelessly.

"He dragged her out of line at the male revue last night at the Jacobsville theater," Misty explained. "We're getting even."

Tyler's eyes widened. "You tried to see a male strip show? Abby!"

Abby glared at him. "Where else do you expect me to get educated? Calhoun wants me to wear diapers for the rest of my life. He doesn't think I'm old enough to go on dates or walk across the street alone."

"You're like a kid sister to him," Tyler said, defending his friend. "He doesn't want you to get hurt."

"I can get hurt if I like," Abby grumbled. Her eyes closed. She was feeling worse by the second, but she couldn't let on. Tyler was as bad as the Ballenger brothers. He'd have her out of here like a shot if he thought she was sick.

"What are you drinking?" Tyler asked, staring at her glass.

"Gin and tonic," she replied, opening her eyes. "Want some?"

"I don't drink, honey," Tyler reminded her with a slow smile. "Well, I've got to pick up Shelby at the office. She had to work late tonight. Watch out for Abby, Misty."

"Of course I will. Sure you won't stay and dance with me?" Misty asked.

Tyler got up, his eyes worried as they trailed over Abby's wan face. "Sorry. I don't usually have to get Shelby, but her car was in the shop today and they didn't finish with it."

"Lucky Shelby, to have a brother like you," Abby mumbled. "I'll bet you don't have a kamikaze pilot fly behind her when she goes to work, or a gang of prizefighters to walk her home after dark, or a whole crew of off-duty policemen to fend off her suitors…."

"Oh, boy," Tyler sighed.

"Don't worry," Misty told him. "She's fine. She's just miffed at Calhoun, that's all. Although how anybody could get upset at a dishy man like that being so protective—"

"Dishy isn't a word I'd use to describe Calhoun if he finds Abby like that and thinks you're responsible for it," Tyler cautioned. "Have you ever seen him get angry?"

Misty pushed back her curly hair uncomfortably. "Justin's temper is worse," she reminded him.

Tyler lifted an eyebrow. "Don't be so sure. They're cut from the same cloth." He touched Abby's shoulder. "Don't drink any more of that." He gestured toward her drink.

"Whatever you say, Ty," Abby said, smiling. "Good night."

"Good night."

He waved and left them there.

"I wonder what he was doing here," Misty said, puzzled. "Since he doesn't drink."

"He may have been looking for somebody," Abby murmured. "I guess a lot of cattlemen congregate around here on the weekends. This stuff is pretty good, Misty," she added, taking another sip.

"You promised you wouldn't," she was reminded.

"I hate men," Abby said. "I hate all men. But especially I hate Calhoun."

Misty chewed her lower lip worriedly. Abby was starting to tie one on, and that wasn't at all what Misty had had in mind. "I'll be back in a minute, honey," she promised, and got up to go after Ty. She had a feeling she was going to need his help to get Abby to the car, and now was the time to do it.

The minute she left, the burly, intoxicated man who'd been watching Abby for the past hour seized his opportunity. He sat down next to her, his small, pale eyes running hungrily over her.

"Alone at last," he drawled. "My gosh, you're a pretty thing. I'm Tom. I live alone and I'm looking for a woman who can cook and clean and make love. How about coming home with me?"

Abby gaped at him. "I don't think I heard you?"

"If you're here with a girlfriend, you've got to be out looking for it, honey." He laughed drunkenly. "And I can sure give it to you. So how about it?" He put his pudgy-fingered hand on her arm and began to caress it. "Nice. Come here and give old Tom a kiss…."

He pulled her toward him. She protested violently, and in the process managed to knock her drink over onto him. He cursed a blue streak and stood up, holding her by the wrist, homicide in his drunken eyes.

"You did that on purpose," he shot at her. "You soaked me deliberately! Well, let me tell you, lady, no broad pours liquor on me and gets away with it!"

Abby felt even sicker. He was hurting her wrist, and there was a deathly hush around them. She knew that most people didn't involve themselves in this kind of conflict. She couldn't fight this man and win, but what else was she going to do? She wanted to cry.

"Let her go."

The voice was deep, slow, dangerous and best of all, familiar. Abby caught her breath as a tall, heavily built blond man came toward her, his dark, deep-set eyes on the man who had Abby's wrist. He was in a gray vested suit and a dressy cream-colored Stetson and boots, but

Abby knew the trappings of civilized company wouldn't save this ruddy cretin if he didn't turn her loose. Abby had seen Calhoun lose his temper, and she knew how hard he could hit when he did.

"What's she to you?" the drunken cowboy demanded.

"My ward."

Calhoun caught the smaller man's wrist in a hard grasp and twisted. The man groaned and went down, holding his hand and cursing.

"Hey, you can't do that to Tom!" one of the man's cronies protested, standing up. He was almost Calhoun's size, and a lot rougher-looking.

"Want to make something out of it, sonny?" Calhoun asked in a soft drawl that was belied by the dark glitter in his eyes.

"You bet I do!"

The younger man threw a punch, but he was too slow. Calhoun's big fists put him over a table. He reached down and picked up the Stetson that the man's blow had connected with and looked around the room as he ran his fingers through his thick, silky blond hair.

"Anybody else?" he invited pleasantly.

Eyes turned the other way, and the band started playing again. Then Calhoun looked down at Abby.

She swallowed. "Hi," she said, and tried to smile. "I thought you were out on a date."

He didn't say a word, but his glittering eyes told her every single thing he was feeling. He wouldn't admit for a minute that his dinner date was strictly business, or that he'd expected something like this after the argument he and Abby had had. She was giving him fits, but he didn't let his expression show how concerned he really was.

"Did you see Misty?" she asked hopefully.

"Luckily for her, no," he said in a tone that could have boiled ice water. "Get your purse."

She fumbled on the chair beside hers for it, weak and shaky. He had a gift for intimidating people, she thought, watching him slam his Stetson over his eyes at a slant. The men who were picking themselves up off the floor didn't seem anxious to tangle with him twice. It was amazing, she thought, how unruffled he looked for a man who'd just been in a fight.

He caught her arm and propelled her out of the bar and into the night air. Misty and Ty were standing just outside, both looking faintly apprehensive.

"It wasn't all my fault, Cal," Misty began in a subdued tone.

Calhoun eyed her coldly. "You know what I think of this so-called friendship. And I know the reason behind it, even if she doesn't."

Abby was puzzled by that remark. The cold, level look in Calhoun's dark eyes and the uncomfortable flush in Misty's pretty face didn't add up.

"I'd better go get Shelby," Ty said quietly. "I was going to offer to take Abby home, but under the circumstances I'm a bit relieved that you came along," he told Calhoun.

"If Justin finds out you were in the same room with her, there'll be hell to pay," Calhoun agreed. "But thanks all the same." He turned Abby toward his Jaguar. "I assume you rode into town with your girlfriend?" he added.

"We came in Misty's car," Abby murmured. She felt weary and a little sick. Now she really looked like a child, with all the concerned adults making a fuss over her. Tears burned in her eyes, which she was careful to keep hidden from the angry man beside her.

"Honest to God," he muttered as he put her into the passenger seat and went around to get into the driver's seat. "I don't know what the hell's wrong with you lately. Last night I find you in line at a male strip show, and tonight you're getting drunk and eyeing strange men in bars!"

"I was not eyeing that lewd creature," she said unsteadily. "And you can't say I was dressed to invite his kind of comment. I'm not wearing anything that's the least bit immodest!"

He glanced at her. "You were in a bar unescorted. That's all the invitation that kind of man needs!"

She felt his gaze on her, but she wouldn't look at him. She knew she'd cry if she did. She clasped her hands firmly in her lap and stared out the window instead as he started the car and headed for home.

It was a long ride, over deserted paved roads and dirt ones that led past the huge feedlot and then uphill to the house, which sat on a level plain about three miles away.

"Do you want me to carry you?" he asked stiffly as he helped her out of the car and she stumbled.

She pushed away from him as if she'd touched hot coals. "No, thank you." He was making her more nervous than ever tonight. The scent of him filled her nostrils, all leathery and spicy and clean. She averted her eyes and walked as straight as she could toward the kitchen door. "Are you going to sneak me in the back way so that Justin doesn't see me?" she challenged.

"Justin told me where to find you," Calhoun said as he put the key in the lock and opened the back door. "He's still watching his war movie."

"Oh." She walked through the door he was holding open for her. "I thought you were out on a date."

"Never mind where I was," he said curtly. "My God, I really must have radar."

She flushed. Thank God he couldn't see her face. She felt odd tonight. Frightened and nervous and a little unsure of herself. The gin had taken away some of her inhibitions, and she had to be careful not to let Calhoun see how vulnerable she felt when he came close to her.

She went in ahead of him, barely noticing the huge, spotless kitchen with its modern conveniences, or the hall, or the mahogany staircase she began to climb. Behind the closed living room door, bombs were going off in a softly muted way, indicating that Justin's war movie was still running.

"Abby."

She stopped, her back to him, trying not to show how nervous she felt. He was behind her, much too close, and she could smell the fresh, clean scent of his body and the spicy cologne he wore.

"What's wrong, honey?" he asked.

His tone broke her heart. He used it with little things—a newborn kitten, or a filly he was working for the first time. He used it with children. He'd used it with Abby the day her mother had died in the wreck. It had been Calhoun who'd found her and broken the news to her and then held her while she cried. It was the tone he used when something was hurt.

She straightened, trying hard to keep her back straight and her legs under control. "That man…" she began, unable to tell him he was breaking her heart because he couldn't love her.

"Damn that drunken—" He turned her, his strong

hands gentle on her upper arms, his dark eyes blazing down into hers. He was so big, and none of it was fat. He was all muscle, lean and powerful, all man. "You're all right," he said softly. "Nothing happened."

"Of course not," she whispered miserably. "You rescued me. You always rescue me." Her eyes closed, and a tear started down her cheek. "But hasn't it occurred to you that I'm always going to land in trouble if you don't let me solve my own problems?" She looked up at him through a mist. "You have to let go of me," she whispered huskily, and her eyes reflected her heartbreak. "You have to, Calhoun."

There was a lot of truth in what she said, and he didn't really know how to respond. He worried about her. This strange restlessness of hers, this urge to run from him, wasn't like Abby. She was melancholy, when for the past five years or more she'd been a vibrant, happy little imp, always laughing and playing with him, teasing him, making him laugh. She couldn't know how somber the house had been when she'd first come to live with him and Justin. Justin never laughed anyway, and Calhoun had come to be like him. But Abby had brought the sunshine. She'd colored the world. He scowled down at her, wondering how she did it. She wasn't pretty. She was plain, and she was serious a good bit of the time. But when she laughed... When she laughed, she was beautiful.

His hands contracted. "I wouldn't mind if you'd go to conventional places," he muttered. "First I catch you in line to watch a bunch of nude men parade around a stage, and the very next night you're drinking gin and tonic in a bar. Why?" he asked, his deep voice soft with curiosity and concern.

She shifted. "I'm just curious about those things," she said finally.

He searched her eyes quietly. "That isn't it," he replied, his own gaze narrowing. His hands shifted, gentle on her arms, Abby could feel their warmth through the fabric. "Something's eating you alive. Can't you tell me what it is?"

She drew in her breath. She'd almost forgotten how perceptive he was. He seemed to see right through to the bone and blood sometimes. She let her gaze drop to his chest, and she watched its lazy rise and fall under his gray vest. He was hairy under his shirt. She'd seen him once in a while on his way to or from the shower, and it had been all she could do not to reach out and run her hands over him. He had thick brown hair across his tanned chest, and it had golden tips where it curled. There was a little wave in his thick blond hair, not much, but enough that it was unruly around his ears. She let her gaze go up, feeding on him, lingering just above his dimpled chin at the thin but sensuous curve of his upper lip and the faintly square, chiseled fullness of his lower lip. He had a sexy mouth. His nose was sexy, too. Very straight and imposing. He had high cheekbones, and thick eyebrows on a jutting brow that shadowed his deep-set eyes. He had black eyes. Both the Ballengers did. But Calhoun was something to look at, and poor old Justin was as rangy-looking as a longhorn bull by comparison.

"Abby, are you listening to me?" Calhoun murmured, shaking her gently because her faintly intoxicated stare was setting his blood on fire.

Her eyes levered up to his, finding darkness in them, secrets, shadows. Her lips parted on a hopeless sigh. When Misty had told her last week about seeing him with some ravishing blonde up in Houston, it had knocked her for a loop, bringing home the true hopelessness of her situation. Calhoun liked sophisticated women. He'd never look twice at drab little Abby. Once Abby had faced that unpalatable fact, she'd been on a one-way road to misery. She'd been looking for an escape, last night and tonight, but she couldn't find one. Wherever she turned, Calhoun was there, hounding her, not realizing how badly he was hurting her.

"What did you say?" she asked miserably.

His chest rose and fell roughly. "It's hopeless trying to talk to you in this condition. Go to bed."

"That's just where I was headed," she said.

She turned and started up the staircase ahead of him, her eyes burning with tears that she was too proud to let him see. Oh, Calhoun, she moaned inwardly, you're killing me!

She went into her room and closed the door behind her. She almost locked it, but realized that would be a joke and a half. Locking a door against Calhoun was a hilarious idea. He'd as soon come looking for a lady vampire as to look at Abby with amorous intent. She started laughing as she went into the bathroom to bathe her face, and she almost couldn't stop.

Chapter 4

Abby managed to get into the silver satin nightgown, but she couldn't seem to fasten it in the front. The gown hung open over her full, firm breasts. She looked at herself in the mirror as she passed it, fascinated by the sophistication the unbuttoned state lent her. She looked oddly mature with the pink swell of her breasts blatantly revealed and her long hair tangled around her face. Then she laughed at her own fancy and stretched out on top of the pale pink coverlet on her canopied bed.

The whole room was decorated in shades of pink and white with blue accents. She loved it. The Ballengers had let her choose her own colors, and these were what she favored. Very feminine colors, even if she wasn't a sophisticated blonde. She shifted restlessly on the cover, and the bodice of her gown came completely away from one breast. Her eyes closed. What did it matter, she thought as she drifted off to sleep. There was no one to see her.

No one except Calhoun, who eased the door open with an expression of concern in his dark eyes. He saw something that knocked the breath out of him.

Abby was barely conscious. She didn't even open her eyes when he came into the room. It was just as well, because he knew he wouldn't be lucid if he had to speak. He'd never thought of Abby as a woman, but the sight of her in that silky drift of silver fabric, with one exquisite breast completely bare and her slender body outlined to its best advantage, shot through him like fire.

He stood frozen in the doorway, facing for the first time the fact that Abby was an adult. No sane man who saw her lying there like that could ever think of her as a child again. And even as the thought formed he realized why he hadn't been himself lately, why he'd deliberately antagonized her, why he'd been so overprotective. He… wanted her.

He closed the door absently behind him and moved closer to her. God, she was lovely! His face hardened as he stared down at her, helplessly feeding on the sensuous nudity she wasn't even aware of.

He wondered if she'd ever let any of her dates see her like this, and a murderous rage stiffened his tall form. He hated the thought of that. Of another man looking at her, touching her, putting his mouth on that soft swell and searching for a tip that he could make hard with the warm pressure of his open mouth….

He shook himself. This wouldn't do. "Abby," he said tersely.

She stirred, but only to shift on the bed so that the whole damned bodice fell open. He actually trembled at the sweetness of her pretty pink breasts with their delicate mauve tips relaxed in sleep.

He muttered something explosive and forced himself

to bend over her, to pull the fabric together and fasten it. His hands shook. Thank God she wasn't awake to witness his vulnerability.

She moaned when his hard knuckles came into contact with her skin, and she arched slightly in her sleep.

His lips parted on a rough breath. Her skin was like silk, warm and sensuous. He gritted his teeth and caught the last button. Then he scooped her up in his arms and stood holding her propped on one knee while he tore the covers loose and stripped back the colorful pink patterned top sheet over the soft blue fitted one.

Her eyes blinked and opened lazily. She searched his hard face, smiling faintly. "I'm asleep," she whispered, nuzzling close. Her sweet scent and the feel of her soft body in his arms overwhelmed him.

"Are you?" he asked, his voice deeper, huskier than he wanted it to be. He laid her down on the sheet, cupping the back of her head in his hand while he drew a pillow under it, his mouth just above hers.

Her hands were around his neck. He drew them down and pulled the covers up over her with a feeling of relief.

"I never had anybody tuck me in before," she mumbled drowsily.

"Don't expect a bedtime story," he murmured, his deep voice lazy with forced humor. "You're too young for the only ones I know."

"I guess I am. Too young for everything. Much too young." She sighed heavily, as her eyes closed. "Oh, Calhoun, I wish I was blond…."

"Now what brought that on?" he asked, but she was asleep again. He looked down at her softly flushed sleeping face, his eyes narrow and dark and thoughtful.

After a minute he turned and went out, flicking off the light behind him.

Justin was coming out of the living room when Calhoun got back downstairs.

"Did you bring Abby home?" Justin asked his brother.

"Yes. She's in bed. Dead drunk," Calhoun added with a faintly amused smile. He'd already taken off his Stetson, along with his jacket and vest.

Justin's dark eyes narrowed. "What's wrong with you? Your lip is cut."

"A slight altercation in the local bar and dance hall," Calhoun said sardonically. He went to the brandy bottle and poured himself half a snifterful. He swirled it, staring into the glass. "Want one?"

Justin shook his head and lit a cigarette instead, ignoring Calhoun's pointed glare of disapproval.

"What were you fighting about?"

Calhoun sipped his brandy. "Abby."

Justin turned, his dark eyebrows arching. "Abby?"

"Misty Davies took her to a bar."

"Last night a nude revue, tonight a bar." Justin stared at his cigarette. "Something's eating our girl."

"I know. I just don't know what. I don't like what Misty's doing, either, but I can't tell Abby."

Justin cocked his head as he drew on the cigarette. "She's trying to get back at you through Abby, I gather."

"Got it in one." Calhoun raised the brandy snifter mockingly before he drained it. "She came on to me hard, and I turned her down. My God, as if I'd be crazy enough to seduce Abby's best friend."

"Misty should have known that. Is Abby all right?"

"I guess," Calhoun said, not adding that he'd put

her to bed himself or that she was the reason he was drinking, something he rarely did. "Some red-faced jackass was manhandling her."

Justin whirled. "And?"

"I think I knocked one of his teeth out."

"Good for you. All the same, she needs watching."

"I'll say amen to that. Shall we flip a coin?" Calhoun asked with pursed lips.

"Why should I interfere when you're doing such a good job of looking out for her interests?" Justin asked, smiling faintly. His smile faded as he searched the younger man's troubled eyes. "You do remember that Abby turns twenty-one in three months? And I think she's already been apartment-hunting with Misty."

Calhoun's face hardened. "Misty will corrupt her. I don't want Abby passed around like an hors d'oeuvre by some of Misty's sophisticated boyfriends."

Justin's eyebrows arched. That didn't sound like Calhoun. Come to think of it, Calhoun didn't *look* like Calhoun. "Abby's our ward," he reminded his brother. "We don't own her. We don't have the right to make her decisions for her, either."

Calhoun glared at him. "What do you want me to do, let her be picked up and assaulted by any drunken cowboy who comes along? Like bloody hell I will!"

He turned on his heel and walked out of the room. Justin pursed his thin lips and smiled softly to himself.

Abby woke the next morning with a headache and a feeling of impending doom. She sat up, clutching her head. It was seven o'clock, and she had to be to work by 8:30. Even now, breakfast would be underway downstairs. Breakfast. She swallowed her nausea.

She got out of bed unsteadily and went into the bathroom to wash her face and brush her teeth. She managed that and felt much better. As she started to get out of her gown, she noticed that the buttons were fastened. Odd. She was sure she'd left the thing unbuttoned. Oh, well, she must have gotten it buttoned and climbed in under the covers sometime before dawn.

It was Saturday, but ordinarily the feedlot stayed open. The cattle still had to be looked after, and the paperwork had to be done no matter what day it was. Abby had gotten used to the long work week, and it was just routine not to have her Saturdays free. She could get off at noon sometimes if she needed to go somewhere. But that hadn't been her habit in recent months. She was hungry for the sight of Calhoun, and he was there most weekends.

She got into a pale gray suit with a blue silk print blouse and put her hair into a French twist. She used a little makeup—not much—and slid her nylon-encased feet into tiny stacked high heels. Well, she was no ravishing beauty, that was for sure, but she wouldn't disgrace herself. She was going down with all flags flying. Calhoun would be mad as fury, and she couldn't let him see how pale she was.

The Ballenger brothers were both at the table when she got downstairs. Calhoun glanced at her, his gaze odd and brooding, as she sat between him and Justin.

"It's about time," he said curtly. "You look like hell, and it serves you right. I'll be damned if I'll have you passing out in bars with that Davies woman!"

"Please, Calhoun, not before I eat," Abby murmured. "My head hurts."

"No wonder," he shot back.

"Stop cussing at my breakfast table," Justin told him firmly.

"I'll stop when you do," Calhoun told his brother, just as firmly.

"Oh, hell," Justin muttered, and bit into one of Maria's fluffy biscuits.

Ordinarily that byplay would have made Abby smile, but she felt too dragged-out to care. She sipped black coffee and nibbled at buttered toast, refusing anything more nourishing.

"You need to take some aspirins before you go to work, Abby," Justin said gently.

She managed to smile at him. "I will. I guess gin isn't really my drink."

"Liquor isn't healthy," Calhoun said shortly.

Justin's eyebrows lifted. "Then why were you emptying my brandy bottle last night?"

Calhoun threw down his napkin. "I'm going to work."

"You might offer Abby a lift," Justin suggested with a strangely calculating expression.

"I'm not going directly to the feedlot," Calhoun said. He didn't want to be alone with Abby, not after the way he'd seen her the night before. He could hardly look at her without remembering her lying across that bed….

"I'm not through with breakfast," Abby replied, hurt that Calhoun didn't seem to want her company. "Besides," she told Justin with a faint smile, "I can drive. I didn't really have all that much to drink."

"Sure," Calhoun replied harshly, dark eyes blazing. "That's why you passed out on your bed."

Abby knew she'd stopped breathing. Justin was pouring cream into his second cup of coffee, his keen eyes on the pitcher, not on the other occupants of the room. And that was a good thing, because Abby looked up at Calhoun with sudden stark knowledge of what he'd seen the night before and had her fears confirmed by the harsh stiffening of his features.

She blushed and started, almost knocking over her cup. So she had gone to sleep on the covers. Calhoun found her with her bodice undone, he'd seen her—

"Never mind breakfast. Let's go," Calhoun said suddenly, his lean hand on the back of her chair. "I'll take you to the feedlot before I do what I have to. You're not fit to drive."

Justin was watching now, his gaze narrow and frankly curious as it went from Abby's red face to Calhoun's taut expression.

That look was what decided Abby that Calhoun was the lesser of the two evils. She couldn't tell Justin what had happened, but he'd have it out of her in two seconds if she didn't make a run for it. Calhoun must have realized that, too.

He took her arm and almost pulled her out of the chair, propelling her out of the room with a curt goodbye to his brother.

"Will you slow down?" she moaned as he took the steps two at a time. "My legs aren't long enough to keep up with you, and my head is splitting."

"You need a good headache," he muttered without a glance in her direction. "Maybe it will take some of the adventure out of your soul."

She glared at his broad back in silence as she followed him to the Jaguar and got into the passenger seat.

He started the car and reversed it, but he didn't go toward the feedlot. He went down the driveway, turned off onto a ranch road that wasn't much more than a rut in the fenced pastures and cut off the engine on a small rise.

He didn't say anything at first. He rested his lean hands on the steering wheel, studying them in silence, while Abby tried to catch her breath and summon enough nerve to talk to him.

"How dare you come into my room without knocking," she whispered after a long minute, her voice sounding husky and choked.

"I did knock. You didn't hear me."

She bit her lower lip, turning her gaze to the yellowish-brown pastures around them.

"Abby, for God's sake, don't make such an issue out of it," he said quietly. "Would you rather I'd left you like that? What if Justin had come to wake you, or Lopez?"

She swallowed. "Well, I guess they'd have gotten an eyeful," she said, her voice unsteady. After a minute, her face flushed, she turned toward him and asked plaintively, "Calhoun...I wasn't uncovered all the way, was I?"

He looked into her eyes and couldn't quite manage to look away. She was lovely. He reached out involuntarily and touched the side of her neck, his fingers tender and exquisitely arousing.

"No," he managed, watching the relief shadow her eyes as he told the lie with a straight face. "I buttoned you back up and tucked you in."

She let out a hard breath. "Thank you."

His fingers moved up to her cheek. "Abby, have you ever let a man see your breasts?" he asked unexpectedly.

She couldn't handle a remark that intimate. She dropped her eyes and tried to catch her breath.

"Never mind, tenderfoot," he chided softly. "I can guess."

"You mustn't talk like that," she whispered.

"Why?" he mused, tilting her chin up so that her shocked eyes met his. "You're the one trying to grow up, aren't you? If you want me to treat you like an adult, Abby, then this is part of it."

She shifted nervously. He made her feel so gauche it was ridiculous. She twisted her purse out of shape, afraid to meet the dark eyes that were relentlessly probing her face.

"Don't," she pleaded breathlessly, and her eyes closed.

"Are you really afraid of me?" he asked, his voice deeper, silkier.

He touched her mouth with a lean forefinger and she actually jumped, her eyes flashing open, all her hidden hungers and fears lying vulnerable there. And that was when his self-control fell away. She was hungry for him. Just as hungry as he was for her. Was that why she'd been so restless, because she'd become attracted to him and was trying to hide it? He had to know.

She couldn't answer him. She felt as if he were trying to see inside her mind. "I'm not afraid of you. Can't we go?"

"What are you trying to do?" he whispered, leaning closer, threatening her lips with his. "Block it out? Pretend that you aren't hungry for my mouth?"

Her heart went wild at the soft question. If he didn't stop, she was going to go in headfirst. He could be playing, and to have him tease her without meaning it would kill her. Her fingers touched his shoulder, pushed experimentally against the hard muscle under the soft fabric of his suit. They trembled there as her eyes suddenly tangled with his and her mouth echoed the faint tremor of her body.

He stared at her. It was a kind of exchange that Abby had never experienced before. A level, unblinking, intense look that curled her toes and made her heart race. Very adult, very revealing. His dark eyes held hers, and his lean fingers traced up and down her soft throat, arousing, teasing. His hard mouth moved closer to hers, hovering above it so that she could feel his warm, minty breath on her parted lips, so that she was breathing him.

"Cal…houn," she whispered, her voice breaking on a hungry sob.

She heard his intake of air and felt his hand curl under her long hair, powerful and warm, cradling her nape to tilt her head up.

"This has been coming for a hell of a long time, baby," he whispered as his head bent and he started to give in to the hunger that had become a fever in his blood. "I want it as much as you do…."

He leaned even closer, but just as his hard mouth started down over hers, before his lips touched her pleading ones, the sound of an approaching vehicle broke them apart like an explosion.

Calhoun felt disoriented. He looked in the rearview mirror and saw one of the ranch trucks coming up behind, but it took a moment to register. He was having trouble breathing. His body felt rigid, like drawn cord.

He glanced at Abby. She'd moved away and the realization that she was trembling brought home the total shock of what he'd been about to do. Damn it, she'd knocked him for a loop without even trying. That made him mad, and so, ironically, did the fact that she'd given in so easily. It infuriated him even more that he'd been about to kiss her. He didn't want complications, damn it, and Abby was the biggest he'd ever faced. Was she vulnerable because she wanted him or just because she'd suddenly discovered that she was a woman and wanted to experiment?

"We'd better get to work," he said tersely, starting the Jaguar. He drove down the path, waving to the men in the vehicle behind them. He cut off at the next dirt road, and minutes later they were at the feedlot. "Go on in. I've got to drive over to Jacobsville and talk to our attorney for a few minutes," he said as coolly as he could. That was a bald-faced lie, but he needed time to get hold of himself. He was as tense as a boy with his first woman, and he was losing his sense of humor. He didn't want Justin to see him like this and start asking embarrassing questions.

"All right," Abby said, her voice faltering.

He glanced at her with narrowed eyes. She'd give the show away all by herself if she went inside looking like that. "Nothing happened," he said shortly. "And nothing will," he added, his voice cold, "if you can manage to stop looking at me like a lovesick calf!"

A sob tore from her throat. Her wide, hurt eyes sought his and quickly fell away. She opened the door and got out, closing it quietly behind her. She straightened and walked toward the office without looking back.

Calhoun almost went after her. He hadn't wanted to say that to Abby, of all people, but he was off balance and terrified of what he might do to her if she kept looking at him that way. He couldn't make love to her, for God's sake. She was a child. She was his ward. Even as he told himself that, a picture formed in his mind of

Abby lying on the bed with her breasts bare. He groaned and jerked the car into gear, sending it flying down the road.

Abby didn't know how she got through the day. It was impossible to act as if nothing had happened, but since Justin knew she had a hangover he didn't question her pale complexion or her unusually quiet demeanor. And Calhoun didn't come back to the office. That was a godsend. Abby didn't think she could have borne seeing him after what he'd said to her.

"You need a diversion," Justin remarked later in the day, just about quitting time. "How about a steak in Houston? I've got to meet a man and his wife to talk about a new lot of stocker calves, and I'd hate to go alone."

He was smiling, and Abby warmed to his gentle affection. Justin wasn't the cold creature most people thought him. He was just a sad, lonely man who should have married and had several children to spoil.

"I'd like that very much," Abby said honestly. It would be nice to go out to dinner, especially if it meant she could avoid Calhoun. Of course, it was Saturday night. He wasn't usually home on Saturday nights anyway, but it would be so much better if she didn't have to dread seeing him.

"Good," Justin said, rising. "We'll get away about six."

Abby wore a soft burgundy velour dress. It had a slightly flared knee-length skirt and bishop sleeves, and a neckline that was V-shaped and not at all suggestive. She wore black accessories with it and, because it had turned cold, her heather-colored wool cape.

"Very nice," Justin said, smiling. He had on dark

evening clothes and looked elegant and sophisticated, as he always did on the rare occasions when he dressed up.

"I could return the compliment," Abby said. She clutched her purse, sending a restless look down the hall.

"He won't be home," Justin told her, intercepting her worried glance. "I gather the two of you had another falling-out?"

She sighed. "The worst yet," she confessed, unwilling to tell him any of the details. She looked up at him. "Calhoun acts as if he hates me lately."

Justin searched her eyes quietly. "And you don't know why," he mused. "Well, give it time, Abby. Rome wasn't built in a day."

She blinked. "I don't understand."

He laughed softly and took her arm. "Never mind. Let's get going."

Houston was big and sprawling and flat as a pancake, but it had a very special personality and Abby loved it. At night it was as colorful as Christmas, all jewel lights and excitement.

Justin took her to a small, intimate dinner club where they met the Joneses, Clara and Henry. They owned a small ranch in Montana where they raised stocker calves to supply to feedlots. They were an older couple but full of fun, and Abby liked them instantly. She and Clara talked fashion while Justin and Henry talked business. Abby was really having a good time until she glanced across the room and saw a familiar face on the cozily intimate dance floor.

Calhoun! Her eyes widened as she followed his blond head through the crowd until there was a clear space. Then she saw the ravishing blonde with him. He was holding the woman, who was at least his own age, with both hands at her waist, and she was curled up against him as if they'd been dancing together for years. They were smiling at each other like lovers.

Abby felt sick. She could almost feel herself turning green. If Calhoun had worked at it for years, he couldn't have hurt her any worse. Coming on the heels of the insulting remark he'd made just a few hours earlier, it was a death blow. This was his kind of woman, Abby realized. Sleek, beautiful, sophisticated. This was one of his shadowy lovers. One of the women he never brought home.

"What's wrong, Abby?' Justin asked suddenly. But before she could answer he followed her gaze to the dance floor, and something in his dark eyes became frightening, dangerous.

"Isn't that Calhoun?" Henry Jones grinned. "Well, well, let's get him over here, Justin, and see what he thinks of our proposition." Before anyone could stop him, he got up and headed for the dance floor.

"Mrs. Jones, shall we go to the powder room?" Abby asked with a pale but convincing smile.

"Certainly, dear. Excuse us, won't you, Justin?" the white-haired woman asked politely, and started out of the restaurant ahead of Abby.

Justin unexpectedly caught Abby's upper arm and drew her back. "Don't panic," he said quietly. "I'll get you out of here as soon as I can. Do you want a drink?"

She looked up, almost in tears at his unexpected understanding. "Could I have a piña colada with just a little rum?" she asked.

"I'll order it. Keep your chin up."

She smiled at him softly. "Thanks, big brother," she said gently.

He grinned. "Any time. Get going."

She glanced away in time to catch Calhoun's dark eyes. She nodded her head at him and turned away with no apparent haste.

Ten minutes later, she and Mrs. Jones returned to find Calhoun about to leave the table, the blonde still clinging to his arm. He looked up at Abby. His face was unreadable, but there was something in his expression that disturbed her. She wasn't about to let it show, though. Lovesick calf, indeed. She'd show him, by gosh.

She smiled. "Hi, Calhoun!" she said easily, sliding into the chair next to Justin's. "Isn't this a nice place? Justin decided I needed a night on the town. Wasn't that sweet of him?" She picked up her piña colada and took a big sip, relieved to find that it had barely enough rum to taste and even more relieved that her hand didn't shake and betray her shattered nerves.

"She's a big girl now," Justin told his brother, leaning back in his chair arrogantly and daring Calhoun to say a word. His cool smile and level, cold stare had a real impact, even on his brother.

But Calhoun didn't look any too pleased at the implication of the remark, especially when Justin slid an arm around Abby's shoulders. In fact, Calhoun seemed almost ready to leap forward and shake his brother loose from Abby.

"I'm tired," the blonde sighed, nuzzling her face against Calhoun's arm. "I need some sleep. Eventually," she teased gently, with a meaningful look at Calhoun's rigid expression.

Abby lifted her chin, looking straight at him. "Enjoy

yourself, big brother," she said with forced gaiety. She even managed a smile. Thank God for Justin. She lifted her glass, took a sip of her drink and winked at the blonde, who smiled at her, obviously thinking Abby was a relative and no threat even if she wasn't.

Calhoun was trying to find his voice. The sight of Abby with his brother was killing him. He hadn't even considered that possibility. And while Justin might not be a playboy, he was a mature, very masculine man, and he had, after all, attracted a beauty like Shelby Jacobs.

Calhoun hadn't meant to ask the blonde out. She was a last-ditch stand against what he was feeling for Abby, and a very platonic one at that. He didn't even want her physically; she was just someone to talk to and be with who didn't threaten his emotions. But he'd never thought Abby might see him with her. It cut him to the bone, embarrassed him. Did Abby care? Try as he might, he couldn't find the slightest hint of jealousy in her face. She was wearing more makeup than usual, and that dress suited her. She looked lovely. Had Justin noticed?

"I said, I'd really like to go home, Cal," the blonde drawled, laughing. "Can we, please? I've had a long day. I'm a model," she added. "And we had a showing this afternoon. My feet are killing me, however unromantic that sounds."

"Of course," Calhoun said quietly. He took her arm. "I'll see you later," he told Justin.

"Sure you will," Justin mused, his tone amused and unbelieving, and he smiled at the blonde, who actually blushed.

Calhoun noticed then how Abby reacted to the remark. She lowered her eyes, but her slender hand was shaking as it held the piña colada. He felt murderous. He wanted to pick her up and carry her out of here, out of Justin's reach.

But Justin had his arm around Abby, and he tightened it. "We may be late," Justin told his brother. "So don't wait up if you beat us home. I thought I might take Abby dancing," he added with narrowed eyes and the arrogant smile Calhoun hated.

"Yes, I'd like that," Abby told him, smiling.

Calhoun felt his throat contracting. He managed a smile, too, but not a normal one. "Good night, then," he said tautly. He hardly heard what the others said as he escorted the blonde out of the restaurant.

"It's all right," Justin told Abby, his voice quiet. "They've gone."

She looked up, her eyes full of tears. "You know, don't you?"

"How you feel, you mean?" he asked gently. He nodded. "Just don't let him see it, honey. He's still got a wild streak, and he'll fight it like hell even if he feels what you do. Give him time. Don't hem him in."

"You know a lot about men," she said, sniffing into the tissue she took from her purse.

"Well, I am one," he replied. "Dry your eyes, now, and we'll take the long way home. That ought to give him hell. He hated the very idea of your being out with me."

"Really?"

He smiled at her expression. "Really. Chin up, girl. You're young. You've got time."

"What do I do in the meantime? He's driving me crazy."

"You might consider looking for that apartment," he

said. "I hate to see you move out, but it may be the only answer eventually."

"I'd already decided that." She wiped her eyes. "But he hates the idea of my rooming with Misty."

"So do I," he remarked honestly. "Did you know that she made a pass at Calhoun and he turned her down?"

"Can't I trust anybody?" she moaned. "Aren't there any women who don't like him?"

"A few, here and there," he mused, his dark eyes twinkling. "I think you might do better to find a room in somebody's house. But that's your decision," he added quietly. "I'm not going to tell you what to do. You're old enough to decide alone."

"Thanks, Justin," she said gently. She smiled. "You'll make some lucky girl a nice husband one day."

His expression hardened, and the humor went out of his dark eyes. "That's a mistake I won't make," he said. "I've had my fill of involvement."

"You never asked about Shelby's side of it," Abby reminded him. "You wouldn't even listen, Calhoun said."

"She said it all when she gave me back the ring. And I don't want to discuss it, Abby," he cautioned, his eyes flashing warning signals as he rose. "I talk to no one about Shelby. Not even you."

She backed down. "Okay," she said gently. "I won't pry."

"Let's go," he said, reaching for the check. "We'll take two hours getting home, and I hope Calhoun has kittens when we get there."

"I doubt he'll notice," Abby said miserably. "She was very pretty."

"Looks don't count in the long run," he replied. He

looked at Abby. "Odd, isn't it, how embarrassed he was when you saw him with her?"

She turned away. "I'm tired. But it was a lovely dinner. Thank you."

He lifted an eyebrow. "Don't thank me. I had a good time. It beats watching movies at home, anyway." He chuckled gently.

Abby wanted to ask him why he never dated anyone and whether he was still carrying a torch for Shelby Jacobs after six years. Calhoun had said he was, but Justin was a clam when it came to his private life. And Abby wasn't about to pry any further. She wasn't that brave, not even with a piña colada inside her.

Chapter 5

Abby was miserable by the time they got home. She'd done nothing but think of Calhoun and the model. Justin had been kind, talking as if she were really listening to him. But she was reliving those few tempestuous minutes in Calhoun's Jaguar, when he'd come so close to kissing her and then had insulted her so terribly. She didn't understand his hot-and-cold attitude or his irritability. She didn't understand anything anymore.

Justin parked his elegant black Thunderbird in the garage, and Abby was surprised to find Calhoun's Jaguar already there.

"Well, well, look who's home," Justin murmured, glancing at Abby. "I guess he felt like an early night."

"Maybe he was exhausted," Abby said coldly.

Justin didn't comment, but he seemed highly amused and smug about something.

Calhoun was in the living room with the brandy

bottle when they got home. He was down to his white shirtsleeves, which he'd rolled up to his elbows. His shirt was almost completely open in front, and Abby had to bite her lip to keep from staring helplessly at the broad expanse of his muscular chest. He was the most sensuous man she'd ever known, so powerful and tall and huge. Just the sight of him made her body tingle.

"So you finally brought her home," Calhoun shot at his brother. "Do you know what time it is?"

"Sure," Justin said imperturbably. "It's two o'clock in the morning."

"What were you doing?"

Justin cocked an eyebrow. "Oh, riding around. And things. Night, Abby," he said, and winked at her before he turned and went up the staircase.

Abby felt as if she'd been poleaxed. Now why had Justin said that? It had made Calhoun look frankly murderous. She cleared her throat.

"I think I'll go up, too." She started to turn, only to have her arm caught by huge warm fingers and be pulled into the living room.

Calhoun slammed the door behind her, his chest heaving with rough breaths. His dark eyes were really black now, glittering, dangerous, and his sensuous mouth was a thin, grim line.

"Where were you?" he demanded. "And doing what? Justin's thirty-seven, and he's no boy."

She stared at him blankly. The sudden attack had knocked the wind out of her for a minute, but then her temper came to the rescue.

"That blonde you were out with was no schoolgirl, either," she replied as calmly as she could, even though her knees were shaking under her. She leaned back against the door for support.

His heavy brows drew together. "My private life is none of your business," he said defensively.

"Of course not," she agreed. "You've already said that you didn't want me hanging around you like a lovesick calf, and I'm doing my best not to," she added, although it hurt terribly to try to make light of that hurtful remark.

His heavy shoulders made a jerky movement as he looked at her and away again, as if her answer made him uncomfortable. "Justin's too old for you."

"Bullfeathers," she replied, lifting her chin. "You've objected to every other man I've ever gone out with, but you can't object to your own brother. Justin would never hurt me, and you know it."

He did know it, but that didn't help. He was dying at the thought of Abby and Justin together.

"Oh, for God's sake!" he burst out, lost for words.

She took a steadying breath, though her heart was still doing a tango in her chest. "Why should it matter to you what I do?" she challenged him. "And you're a fine one to sit in judgment on other people! My gosh, Calhoun, everybody in the world knows what a playboy you are!"

He glared at her, trying to keep his temper. "I'm not a playboy," he said tersely. "I may date women occasionally—"

"Every night," she returned. Even though she knew her assertion wasn't completely true, she was too angry to split hairs. "Not that I mind," she added with a cold smile. "I don't care who you go out with, as long as you stop poking your nose into my business. I'll date whom I please, Calhoun, and if you don't like it, you know what you can do!"

He started to tell her what she could do, but before

he could get the words out she'd jerked the door open and gone out and up the staircase.

"If you stay out until two o'clock in the morning again, with or without Justin, you'll regret it!" Calhoun yelled up the stairs.

Abby made a sound that almost drove him crazy. He muttered something obscene and went back into the living room, slamming the door so hard it shook the room.

Damn women! He could have screamed at the effect she was having on him lately. She was ruining his love life, ruining his business life. All he did was think about her damned pretty breasts....

Abby cried herself to sleep. It had been a rotten evening altogether, and every time she thought of Calhoun kissing that model she got sicker. She hated him. She hated every bone in his body, and she most especially hated his possessiveness. She had to find an apartment. She had to get away. After tonight it was going to be just plain horrible trying to stay in the same house with Calhoun until her birthday.

The next morning she slept late. She usually got up and went to church, but this time she played hooky. She didn't want to risk running into Calhoun.

But as it was, there was nothing to worry about. When she finally went downstairs at lunchtime, wearing jeans and a beige knit top, her hair in a ponytail, Calhoun was nowhere in sight.

"Good morning," Justin said from the head of the table, smiling faintly. "How did it go last night?"

"Don't ask," she groaned. She sat down and glanced nervously at the door. "Is he here?"

He shook his head and filled his cup with coffee then passed the carafe to Abby. "He's still asleep," he said.

That was surprising, because Calhoun was usually up early. Justin actually grinned then. "What happened?"

"He thinks I should be in before two o'clock in the morning, even if he isn't," she said calmly. "And you're too old for me," she added with a faint grin, eyeing him.

He chuckled. "What else?"

"He's going crazy, Justin," she said. "I don't know what's gotten into him lately. It can't be his love life— his model seemed to be more than willing," she added cattily.

Justin looked at her, but he didn't reply. He poured cream into his coffee. "Oh, I almost forgot. Misty phoned. Something about having an apartment she wanted you to look at today if you want to go with her."

"Yes, I think I do," she murmured with a cold glance at the staircase.

"You know I don't approve of Misty as your prospective roommate," Justin told her honestly. "But it's your decision."

"You're a nice man."

"I'm glad you think so. Obviously my brother thinks I'm as big a rake as he is." He chuckled.

"Thank God you aren't," she sighed. "One in the family is enough!"

"If you're going out, you'd better wear a jacket," Justin warned. "I stepped out to get the paper and almost froze in place."

Abby sighed again. "And they keep saying spring is just around the corner."

She finished her breakfast and called Misty to tell her she'd be right over. Then she returned to her room to get her burgundy velour jacket. She was looping the last button when she turned to the open door and found Calhoun standing there, looking at her broodingly.

He'd just showered. He was bare chested, and his blond hair was damp. But Abby's eyes stopped at his brawny chest in helpless appreciation of the sheer masculinity of him. He leaned idly against the doorjamb, and muscles rippled under the wedge of thick brown hair that ran down into the wide belt around his slender hips. He didn't smile, and his dark eyes had heavy circles underneath them. He looked as tired as Abby felt.

"Where are you going now?" he asked coldly.

"Out to look at apartments," she said carelessly. "In a little over two and a half months I'll be needing one."

"How does Justin feel about that?" he asked, his eyes narrowing angrily.

"Justin isn't the one who's trying to keep me in a cage," she replied. She was tired of the whole thing, of his unreasonable anger and even of Justin playing cupid. "Look, Justin just took me out for a meal. He didn't park the car and try to make love to me. He isn't that kind of man, and you should be ashamed of yourself for thinking he is. Justin's like a brother to me. Just…as you are," she finished, averting her eyes. "I don't have romantic thoughts about either one of you."

"And that's a damned lie," he said in a cold tone. He jerked away from the door, slamming it behind him, bringing her shocked eyes to him as he advanced toward her. "I'm no more your brother than I'm your great-uncle."

She backed up into a chair, swerved and made it to the wall. He looked dangerous, and she didn't know how to handle this lightning mood switch.

"That's what you want me to be," she said accusingly,

pressing against the cold wall. "You want me to be a kid sister and not get in your way or make eyes at you—"

"My God, I don't know what I want anymore," he ground out as he placed his big hands on either side of her head, his body too close, too sensuous, too deliciously masculine. The scent of him filled her nostrils, excited her senses. She could see the tiny golden tips of the hair on his chest now, glittering in the light. Glittering…like the dark, intent eyes that caught hers and held them.

"Calhoun, I have to go," she said, her voice faltering.

"Why?" he asked.

She could see him breathing. His chest rose and fell roughly, as if he were having a hard time getting air in and out. She felt that way herself. He was too close, and her vulnerability was going to start showing any minute. She couldn't bear to have him see her weakness and make fun of it.

"Stop it," she whispered huskily, closing her eyes. "Damn you, stop…oh!"

He had her mouth under his so smoothly and easily that her heart seemed to stop beating. He wasn't gentle, either. It was as if the feel of her soft body under his made him wild, made him hungry.

In fact, he was starving for her. He leaned down so that his hips and thighs were fully against her, so that his bare chest was against the velour of her jacket. He didn't like not being able to feel her breasts, so he snapped open the buttons of the jacket and pushed the material aside. He felt her gasp as her breasts pressed against him, and he groaned, marveling at the warm softness of her. Nudging her lips apart, he nipped sensuously at the lower one. That was arousing, too, and he wanted her. He wanted her mouth as he wanted her soft, sweet young body. His tongue pushed into her mouth, past her lips, tangling with her own, and he groaned and gave her his full weight, pressing her against the wall.

Abby was frightened. She hadn't expected anything quite so adult, and she'd never been kissed by anyone who had any expertise. Calhoun was experienced, and he was kissing her as if she knew all the answers, too. But she didn't. The feel of his body in such unfamiliar intimacy was embarrassing, and his mouth was doing shocking things to her own. She pushed at his chest, afraid of his lack of control.

"No!" she whimpered.

He barely heard her. His mind was spinning, his body in torment. He managed to lift his head, breathing roughly, and look down at her. But the passion and delight he had expected to see in her pale eyes was missing. They were wide, but not with desire. With… fear!

He scowled. Her hands were on his chest, but they were pushing, not caressing, and she was crying.

"Abby," he whispered gently. "Honey…"

"Let me…go," she sobbed brokenly. "Oh, let me go!" She pushed again, harder.

This time he flexed his hands against the wall and pushed away from her, leaving her cold, empty. She moved past him, putting half the length of the room between them. So that—that!—was what passion felt like. She shivered a little at the memory. Her mouth hurt where his had ground against it, and her breasts were sore from the hard pressure of his chest. He hadn't even tried to be gentle. She stared at him accusingly, her eyes bright with tears as she drew her jacket closer and shivered.

Calhoun felt as if he'd been hit in the head with a

hammer. Her reaction hadn't been anything like what he'd expected. He'd almost kissed her once before, and she'd been yielding then, willing. But now she looked as if she hated him.

"You hurt me," she whispered shakily.

He was lost for words. Concerned, he stared at her, his dark eyes quiet on her wan face. She looked as if she had never experienced a man's passion. Was that possible? Could any woman be that unawakened in this day and age?

"Haven't you ever been kissed?" he asked softly.

"Of course I have," she replied stiffly. "But not…not like that!"

His eyebrows went up. At last he was catching on. "My God," he said huskily. "Abby, adults kiss that way!"

"Then I don't want to be an adult," she returned, coloring. "Not if I have to be mauled like that!"

He watched her turn and leave the room, and he was powerless to stop her. Her reaction had floored him completely. He'd expected her to know a little about lovemaking, at least, but she seemed totally innocent. She'd never known a deep kiss or the intimacy of a man's body.

It should have pleased him, but he found it irritating that she thought he'd mauled her. By God, he should have let her go out with Myers. Then she'd know what it was to be mauled!

He left the room and closed the door, his expression thunderous as he heard her footsteps going down the staircase and then her muffled goodbye to Justin.

Calhoun went back to his own room. He was breathing roughly, and his heart wouldn't beat properly. He felt hot all over. Frustrated. Furious. Damn Abby and her soft body. It was driving him out of his mind!

He went into the bathroom and turned on the shower. Well, it was a good thing she didn't like his kisses, because hell would freeze over before she ever got another one.

Abby was blissfully unaware of Calhoun's thoughts. She climbed into her car and started it with hands that were still trembling. How could Calhoun have hurt her like that if he'd cared anything about her? He'd just proved how little she meant to him. He'd only been interested in his own pleasure, not hers. Well, he could go back to his blondes for all she cared. She was sure she hated him now.

Misty was already dressed and waiting when Abby got to the colonial mansion the older girl shared with her parents. Misty took them to town in her little sports car, and for once Abby didn't mind the wind. It might blow away her misery. Just thinking about Calhoun's rough treatment made her miserable. She loved him and it hurt terribly that he could treat her that way. But she had to pretend that nothing was wrong, so that Misty wouldn't start asking questions that Abby didn't want to answer.

They parked in town and went to the first address on Misty's list. It was an apartment above a sweet shop, on the corner across from the bank. Misty didn't like the place, because there was only one bedroom and she wanted her privacy. Abby deliberately put the implications of that remark in the back of her mind and added that she didn't like the view. It was too close to the center of town, and there was a good deal of traffic on Saturday night.

The second place they went was just right. The room

being rented was upstairs in a private house owned by a Mrs. Simpson, who was friendly and bright and welcoming. That turned Misty off completely. She didn't want an old busybody watching out for her. But Abby was rapidly coming to the conclusion that Misty was going to do some entertaining once they were on their own, and her association with the Ballengers made her balk at the thought of Misty's plans.

"I'll take it," she told Mrs. Simpson, "if you don't mind having just me instead of both of us, and if you aren't in a hurry for me to move in. It will be a few weeks…."

"That will work out fine. I'm going off to my sister's for a week or so, anyway." Mrs. Simpson smiled broadly, her blue eyes lighting up. "My dear, I'd be delighted." She leaned forward while Misty was still upstairs grumbling about the lack of privacy. "Your friend seems very nice, mind you, but I'm rather old-fashioned…."

"So am I," Abby whispered, putting her finger to her lips when Misty came downstairs again.

"No, I'm sorry, it won't do," she sighed.

"I have the perfect solution," Abby told her. "I'll take this one, and you take the other one. It'll be great. We can visit each other, and we'll both have our privacy."

Misty raised an eyebrow. "Well…it might be nice at that. But you said you wanted to room with me."

Mrs. Simpson excused herself, asking Abby to phone her later about a date for moving in.

Abby moved with Misty to the door. "Let's face it," she told her friend, "you want to entertain men, and I'll have Calhoun and Justin all over me if they find out about it. I'm sure you don't want them on your case."

Misty shuddered delicately. "Are you kidding?

Calhoun, maybe, but not Justin! That man doesn't have a humorous bone in his whole body."

Abby remembered how amused Justin had been about Calhoun's behavior, but she just nodded her head.

"Let's have coffee," Misty suggested. She drove them back into town in her little sports car and parked beside the bank. The two women had just gotten out of the car when Tyler Jacobs and his sister Shelby came around the corner looking somber and disturbed.

Abby greeted them. "Tyler. Shelby. How are you?"

"This isn't a good time to ask," Shelby sighed, but she smiled. She was a dish. Short dark hair framed her elfin face, and she had eyes that were an odd shade of green, almost glassy in color. Her mouth was perfect, and she was tall. She would have made a fortune as a model, but her parents wouldn't have heard of such a profession for their only daughter.

Tyler was like his sister in coloring. He had thick dark hair, almost black, and an olive complexion and the same odd-colored green eyes. He was as big as Calhoun, but slender. Whipcord-lean and dangerous-looking. He wasn't handsome at all, but he had character, and women usually found him irrestible.

Misty turned to see where Abby had gotten to and smiled delightedly at Tyler.

"Well, hello," she drawled. "Fancy seeing you here."

"Hello, Misty," he said, smiling lazily. "You look devastating, as usual. What are you two doing in town on a Sunday?"

"Looking for an apartment to share, originally." Abby sighed. "But we wound up with one each, across town from the other. I'm renting from Mrs. Simpson, and Misty has a neat place overlooking the bank."

"Right up there, in fact." Misty pointed across the street. "It needs decorating, but I can take care of that."

Abby grinned. "I'll bet you can."

"Come and have coffee with us," Shelby invited. "Tyler needs cheering up. We had a bad blow yesterday, and an even worse one today."

Abby looked up at him. He did seem reticent. And moody, which was totally unlike him. "I'm sorry. Can I help?"

"You little doll," he murmured, and touched her hair gently. "No. But thanks for the offer. How's Calhoun?"

Abby averted her eyes. "He's fine, I guess. He and Justin are both at home."

"No problems the other night after Calhoun got you home?" Tyler persisted with a teasing smile.

"Only the usual lecture," Abby said. She managed a shaky smile as all four of them went down the street and entered a small cafeteria.

They were quickly seated, and the waitress brought four cups of coffee and a pitcher of cream.

Shelby cast a glance at Abby and laughed softly. "You devil," she teased.

"I just wanted to see how the other half lived," Abby sighed.

"I did my best to help you," Misty sighed. "On the other hand, weren't you lucky that it was Calhoun and not Justin who came after you? Calhoun is a little more easygoing."

"Not lately, he isn't," Abby said tautly.

At the mention of Justin, Shelby became quiet and shy. Abby felt sorry for her. Justin had never gotten over

Shelby's defection. He probably never would, and Shelby had to know that.

"How is Justin?' Tyler asked casually. Too casually.

"He goes to work and comes home and goes to work and comes home," Abby said as they added cream and sugar to their coffee.

Misty yawned. "What an exciting life."

"He's lonely, I suppose," Abby said deliberately. "He never goes anywhere."

"I know somebody else like that," Tyler murmured with a hard glance at Shelby, who shifted restlessly in her seat.

"How's the horse business going?" Abby interrupted, posing the question to Tyler as she sipped her coffee.

"Going bust, I'm afraid," he said heavily. "Dad made some bad investments before he died. So far, I've managed to meet the payments. This month I defaulted." His face hardened. "I'm going to have to sell Geronimo."

"Oh, Tyler, I'm sorry." Abby grimaced. "He was your favorite."

"Mine, too," Shelby said with a sigh. "But we can't keep him and pay off Dad's debts. I don't suppose you'd want him, Abby?"

"I don't ride that well," Misty confessed.

"If I can talk Justin into it I'd like to have him," Abby said gently.

"Thank you, Abby, but that wouldn't be a good idea," Shelby replied. "Justin would go right through the roof if you asked him."

"Like a rocket," Tyler said, smiling at Abby. "No, we'll do it through an agent. We won't have any problems selling him. I'd rather know who he was going to, that's all. Some people want a horse strictly for breeding purposes. They look at dollars and cents, not at the horse itself."

"I've got a cousin in Texas," Misty piped up. "She's trying to hold on to the ranch all by herself. It's a horse ranch," she added. "Does that tell you anything?"

He smiled. "Enough. I'd appreciate it if you'd put her in touch with me."

"I'll give her your number, if you don't mind."

"Fine."

Lights gleamed in Shelby's black hair as she lifted the cup and finished her coffee. Abby wondered at her elfin beauty, and thought it strange that a man like Justin could attract such a lovely woman when he wasn't handsome or even very personable. Then Abby remembered how kind he'd been to her in Houston, and the way he'd supported her with Calhoun. On the other hand, maybe it wasn't so surprising that he could attract her. What was surprising was that he'd ever let her go. It made Abby uncomfortable, thinking about how two people could be so much in love one day and bitter enemies the next. Love didn't last, after all.

"Tyler, we'd better go. I've got to call Barry Holman about those bonds and securities we're selling," Shelby said gently. "I'm sorry. I'd love to stay and talk. We hardly ever see each other these days, and I guess Justin would burn the house to the ground before he'd let me through the front door to visit you."

Tyler sighed. "He holds a grudge longer than any man I've ever known, that's for sure. And without reason."

"No," Shelby pleaded, her green eyes seeking his. "Please don't. Abby owes him her loyalty. Don't put her in the position of having to defend him."

"Sorry," he said, his green eyes glittering with

controlled rage. Then he smiled at Abby. "There's a square dance at the dance hall next Friday night. How about going with me?"

Abby hesitated. Justin would be furious, and she didn't like to think about what Calhoun might say or do. He was so unpredictable lately. On the other hand, going out with Tyler would show Calhoun that she wasn't going to make eyes at him any more....

"Don't do it," Shelby pleaded. "Can't you see, it will only make things worse."

"For whom?" Tyler shot back. "Could the situation possibly be any worse for you? My God, you're living like a nun!"

Shelby put her napkin down with calm, steady fingers. "The way I live is no one's concern except my own." She stood up. "Abby, Justin would come down on your head like Judgment. He isn't the man he was. I'd hate to see you caught in the cross fire."

"I'm not afraid of him, Shelby," Abby said gently. "Not much, anyway. I'm trying to get out from under Calhoun's thumb. Tyler and I would kind of be helping each other."

"You see," Tyler told his sister. "And here you were thinking I was just doing it to irritate your ex-fiancé."

"Well, aren't you?" Shelby said challengingly.

He lifted his chin arrogantly. "Maybe."

"Sometimes I wonder if Mom and Dad didn't find you under a cabbage leaf," Shelby muttered.

"Not a chance," Misty mused, looking him up and down. "He's much too big."

"Tease," he said, flirting lazily with Misty as he did with most women. But Tyler was deep, like Shelby, and if there was a special woman, nobody knew except himself. He was discreet about his love life.

"Justin used to laugh, you know," Shelby told Abby as they walked out together, with Misty and Tyler talking together ahead of them. "He wasn't always cold and hard and unyielding. Not until I gave him back his ring and made him bitter." She clutched her purse against her breasts. "Abby, don't hurt him," she pleaded, her eyes soft and gentle. "Don't let Tyler hurt him. He hides it, but he's so vulnerable…."

"I know that," Abby said gently. She touched the taller woman's arm, stung by the look in Shelby's eyes. Yes, she was vulnerable, too, and Abby sensed that Shelby was still in love with Justin, even now…. "I'm sorry that things have gone so badly for both of you. Justin doesn't have women, you know. If you live like a nun, he lives like a monk. There isn't anyone."

Shelby's lower lip trembled. She looked away, her head tilting to stop a tear from escaping. "Thank you," she managed huskily.

Abby wanted to say more, but the others were waiting impatiently. "Ready to go?" she called brightly to Misty. "Okay. Can you keep it under ninety going home? Honest to goodness, I don't think that car knows any legal speeds!"

"I'm a good driver," Misty informed her haughtily. "You just come with me and I'll prove it. So long, Tyler. Shelby."

"I'll pick you up at six on Friday," Tyler told Abby. "Wear something sexy."

She curtsied. "You'd better bring a baseball bat when you come to the door. And pray that Justin doesn't have a long cord for his chain saw."

"Dangerous games, my friend," Misty told Abby as they drove away. "Justin won't like it, and he's pretty frightening when he loses his temper."

"So is Tyler. But they won't come to blows. I'll make sure of it."

"And what will Calhoun say?" Misty added with a quick glance at Abby.

Abby felt herself going pale. She could feel all over again the terrible crush of his mouth, the shattering intimacy of his body. She swallowed. "He won't care," she said coldly.

"Why do it? You're moving out. Isn't that enough of a show of independence for you?"

"No." Abby leaned back against the leather seat and closed her eyes. "But going out with Tyler will be."

Misty sighed and shook her head. "Well, I'll remember you in my prayers. Hang on." She pressed her foot down on the accelerator, and Abby wondered what the Guinness book of world records listed as the top land speed by a wild blonde in a little sports car. Whatever the record was, she thought as she held on for dear life, she'd bet that Misty could break it.

Chapter 6

Calhoun was gone when Abby got home, and she spent a quiet afternoon watching television. Justin was around long enough to ask about the apartment and to approve Abby's choice of lodgings. But then he left to deal with some problem at the feedlot.

Abby dreaded the moment when Calhoun would return, because of what had happened that morning. She couldn't reconcile the man she knew with the stranger who'd been so rough with her. Boys had kissed her before, but lightly and carefully. Calhoun hadn't been careful, and he'd frightened her with his experience. She'd never experienced adult passion before, and she didn't know what it was. But surely a man like Calhoun, with his love life, couldn't have been thrown off balance so completely by a twenty-year-old virgin.

He'd already said he didn't want her making eyes at him, so maybe he was showing her what she'd be inviting if she let him see her interest. She shivered. What a deft and accurate way he'd picked, if that were the case.

Supper was on the table and she and Justin were about to start serving themselves when Calhoun came in. He sat down, looking worn and rumpled, and poured himself a cup of coffee. He didn't speak to Abby, and she kept her head down so that he wouldn't notice her scarlet flush. It wasn't necessary, anyway, because he didn't even look at her. He started talking to Justin about a prospective new feedlot customer he'd found, and he kept the conversation going until they were having a second cup of coffee. Abby felt shut out and ignored. When Calhoun finally got up to leave and looked at her, she felt worse than she had in her life.

There was barely controlled anger in his eyes, mingled with something darker, something she didn't understand. She dropped her eyes and felt her heart race under his cold scrutiny. He acted as if she were the guilty one. Didn't he realize how he'd hurt her? That his treatment of her had been frightening?

"Hey," Justin said softly as the outside door opened and closed.

She looked up, her eyes faintly misty. "He didn't even speak to me," she whispered.

Justin leaned back in his chair and lit a cigarette, exhaling smoke as he watched her. "He's been like that all day," he said. "While you were gone he stared out the window whenever I tried to talk to him. He didn't even hear me. Finally he lit a cigarette and went outside and just walked."

She stared at him. "Calhoun stopped smoking years ago."

He shrugged. "He's gone through a pack already.

You keep telling me that there's nothing wrong, but my brother goes from bad to worse. Now either you tell me or I'll beat it out of him. I love him, but I've had enough silence."

Abby swallowed hard. Justin's tone was unnerving. But she couldn't tell him what Calhoun had done. Justin was unpredictable, and she didn't want him to rake Calhoun over the coals for something that in all honesty she'd helped to provoke.

Then she remembered what she'd said to Calhoun, and suddenly all the pieces of the puzzle fit together. She must have hurt Calhoun's pride with what she'd said and done after he'd kissed her so intimately. The more she thought about it, the worse she felt. For months she'd dreamed of having him kiss her. Then he had, and she'd been too frightened by his experienced bulldozer technique to even respond. She'd behaved like a child.

Justin lifted an eyebrow and waited expectantly. When she didn't say anything, he prodded, "Well?"

"I said some terrible things to him," she confessed finally. "I was jealous."

"And hurt," he said perceptively.

"And hurt," she sighed. Her blue-gray eyes met his dark ones. "Oh, Justin, he hates me. And I can't even blame him. I hurt his pride so badly that I don't imagine he'll ever talk to me again."

"Incredible, isn't it, that you could hurt him," he mused. "When women have been trying for years to get through that thick hide and never have."

"He's been responsible for me for a long time," she said quietly. "I guess it's hard for him to let go."

"Maybe," he said. He took another draw on the cigarette. "Maybe not. He's acting strangely lately."

"Maybe he's got the gout or something," she suggested with a slight smile.

"Or something."

She sipped her coffee so that she'd have something to do with her hands. She had to talk to Justin about Friday night, and it was only just dawning on her how difficult it was going to be.

"Justin, I have to tell you something."

His dark eyebrows lifted. "This sounds serious," he said with a faint smile.

"It is. And I hope you won't get mad at me."

His chin lifted. "Is it about the Jacobses?"

"I'm afraid so," she sighed. She looked at her coffee, because his eyes were getting darker by the second. "Tyler asked me to a square dance Friday night, and I said I'd go." She clenched her teeth, waiting for the outburst. When it didn't come, she looked up. He was watching her, but without any particular anger. She continued quickly, "I don't have to let him pick me up here. I can meet him at the dance. In fact, Shelby did her best to stop him from asking me, because she didn't want to upset you."

Something passed across his face, too fleeting to identify. But for one wild second his eyes were soft and quiet and full of wonder. Then it was gone, and he stared down at his glowing cigarette. "Did she?"

"She didn't want Tyler to make any trouble," Abby said gently.

"It's been six years," he said after a minute, his face quiet and oddly gentle. "Six long, empty years. I've hated her, and I've hated the family. I guess I could go on hating them until we're all dead. But it wouldn't change anything. It's all over and done with, a long time ago."

"She's so lovely," Abby said.

Justin winced, and there were memories in his dark eyes, in his taut face. He crushed out his cigarette roughly. "Tyler can pick you up here," he said abruptly, and got to his feet. "I won't give him a hard time."

She looked up as he passed by her chair and then down at her cup, thoughtfully. "She lives like a nun, you know. Tyler says she hasn't dated anyone for years."

Abby thought he stopped then, just for a second, but it might have been her imagination, because he kept walking and he didn't say a word.

What a pity, Abby thought with quiet melancholy, that love could die so violent a death. And the saddest part of it was that in spite of what Justin said, she'd have bet Justin and Shelby were still madly in love, even though it had been six years since they'd broken up. What had Shelby done to make Justin turn against her so vehemently? Surely just being given back his engagement ring wouldn't make a man so vindictive!

Abby got up from the table and went to her room. It was much too early to go to bed, but she didn't relish the idea of staying downstairs and having Calhoun stare holes through her. Avoiding him had suddenly become imperative.

That wasn't too hard. But avoiding the memories that lingered in her room was. The wall where he'd pinned her with his big body and kissed the breath out of her was all too empty. In the end she pushed a bookcase against it, just to keep her mind from replaying the scene.

She went to work as usual for the rest of the week, and so did Calhoun. But there was a difference. There was no soft greeting, no smile, no teasing grin. This Calhoun was more and more like his older brother.

The fun had gone out of him, leaving behind a hard, formidable businessman who alternately ignored Abby or chewed her out for any nervous mistakes she made. It was impossible to get near him, even to talk.

By quitting time on Friday, she was a nervous wreck. She looked forward to the square dance like a doomed prisoner coveting an appeal. At least the dance would get her out of the house and take her mind off Calhoun. Not that she expected him to be home on a weekend. He'd probably be up in Houston with his model. Abby gritted her teeth as she thought about that.

Hindsight was a sad thing, Abby reflected, and she'd only begun to realize why Calhoun had been out of control with her in the bedroom. It hadn't been because he was angry or because he was punishing her. He'd been out of control because he'd wanted her. She was almost sure of it now, having asked Misty some subtle but intimate questions about men. Calhoun had wanted her, and she'd stabbed his pride bloody. She could have cried, because she'd had his attention and hadn't even known it. He was well and truly cured now. He didn't speak to her unless he had to, and he avoided her like the plague. She was glad she'd had that room reserved at the boarding house, because she had a feeling she was going to need it any time now.

She dressed in a red-checked full skirt with several crinolines and a perky white blouse with puffy short sleeves and a button front. It was almost March, but it was still cold, and she got out her long tan coat to wear with it. Tyler was due at six, and it was almost that when she went downstairs, her long hair silky and clean around her shoulders, wearing just enough makeup to give her a rosy-cheeked glow. She'd never wished more that she was blond or that she could have a second chance with

Calhoun. Just her luck, she thought miserably as she made her way down the staircase, to foul everything up on the first try. Why hadn't she realized that Calhoun felt passion, not anger? Why hadn't she waited to give him a chance to be tender? He probably would have been if she hadn't struggled with him.

She reached the bottom of the staircase just in time to watch Calhoun open the front door for Tyler, because Maria and Lopez had the night off. Abby's heart jumped helplessly at the sight of those broad shoulders and that long back. Calhoun was so big he even towered over Tyler.

Abby's body tensed as she wondered if Justin had told Calhoun she'd be going out with Tyler. But he finally opened the door all the way and let the other man inside.

Tyler, in jeans and a red checked Western shirt and bandanna and denim jacket, looked as Western as a man could get, from his black boots to his black hat. Calhoun was dressed in a similar fashion, except that his shirt was blue. They stared at each other for a long moment before Calhoun broke the silence.

"Justin said you were taking Abby out," he said tersely. "You can wait in the living room if you like."

"Thanks," Tyler said, equally tersely, as he met Calhoun's eyes and glanced away.

"I'm already dressed," Abby said with forced cheerfulness, smiling at Tyler and getting a smile back. She didn't look at Calhoun. She couldn't. It would have been like putting a knife in her heart.

"Then let's go," Tyler replied. "I hear the Jones boys are going to play tonight. You remember Ted Jones, Calhoun; he was in our senior class back in high school."

"I remember him," Calhoun said quietly. There was a smoking cigarette in his hand, and he looked like a stranger.

A minute later, Justin came out of his study, stopping short when he saw the three of them. He and Calhoun were wearing almost identical clothing, and it was odd for Justin to dress up on a Friday night. Unless…

"Where are you off to?" Abby asked the oldest of the three men with a smile.

"The square dance, of course," Justin said, glancing at Tyler. "Not to keep tabs on her, in case you were wondering," he added with a cold smile. "We're meeting a business contact there."

Abby's heart jumped. Calhoun was going to the dance, too. She hated her own helpless pleasure at the thought that she might have at least a few minutes in his arms.

Tyler studied Justin warily. "You aren't meeting Fred Harriman, by any chance?"

Justin's eyebrows arched. "Yes. Why?"

Tyler grimaced. "He just bought our place."

Calhoun caught his breath. "For God's sake, you weren't forced out?"

"I'm afraid so," Tyler replied with a sigh. "Funny, you never think you'll go under. I was sure that I could undo the damage Dad had done, but I was too late. At least it's not a complete loss. We've still got a couple of stallions, and we can hold on to at least the house and an acre or two of land."

"If you need a job, we've got one open at the feedlot," Justin said unexpectedly. "It's not charity, damn it," he added when he saw Tyler's incredulous look and glinting green eyes. "I don't have to like you to know how good you are with livestock."

"That's a fact," Calhoun agreed, raising a cigarette to his chiseled mouth. "The door's open."

Abby, watching them, was struck by the sheer force of so much masculinity at close range. The three of them were like patterns cut from the same rough cloth. Long, tall Texans. She was suddenly proud to be a friend to two of them, even if the third hated her.

"Thanks for the offer, then," Tyler said. He stared at Justin. "I didn't think you went to dances, business or not."

"I don't. Calhoun gets drunk if I don't baby-sit him," he said, grinning at his brother's outraged expression.

"Like hell I do," Calhoun replied. "I remember a night when you tied one on royally and I put you to bed."

Justin pursed his lips. "We all lose our heads occasionally," he said. "Don't we, Abby?" he added with a glance in her direction and then in Calhoun's. Abby flushed, and Calhoun turned his back and headed for the front door, holding it open for the rest of them without another word. Justin only smiled.

"Shelby's going, too," Tyler remarked to Abby as they walked out. "I had to twist her arm, but she needs some diversion. She's working a six-day week for the first time in her life, and it's rough."

Justin didn't say a word, but if that quiet unblinking gaze meant what Abby thought it did, he was listening intently. She wondered just how many fireworks a dance hall could stand. Behind her, Calhoun was glaring at her and at Tyler with a scowl so hot that she would have grown warm if she'd seen it.

The dance hall was jumping. The Jones boys' band was playing a toe-tapping Western medley, and the dance floor was full. Old Ben Joiner, his fiddle in his hand, was calling the dance, his voice rising deep and clear above the music as he told the dancers what to do and when.

"Nice crowd," Tyler remarked. He and Abby had arrived after Justin and Calhoun. The two of them were at a table with a third man who looked pitifully out of place.

"Yes, it is nice. What do the brothers want with Fred Harriman, I wonder?" she asked, thinking out loud as she and Tyler headed toward the table where Shelby was sitting all alone.

"You're in a position to know better than I am," Tyler returned, "but I expect he wants the brothers to feed out his new cattle for him." Tyler glanced at his sister and saw where her big, soulful green eyes were staring. "God, she's got it bad," he said under his breath.

Abby noticed, too, and touched his sleeve. "Justin doesn't date, either. Do you suppose there's any chance for them?"

"Not after what he thinks she did," Tyler replied tersely. "And talking about it won't butter any biscuits. Hi, sis," he said more loudly, smiling at his sister as he pulled out a chair for Abby and then sat down himself.

"Hi," Shelby said with a grin. "Abby, you look gorgeous."

"So do you." Abby sighed. "You don't know what I'd give to be as pretty as you are."

"Oh, go on," Shelby murmured, embarrassed. But she did look pretty, her dark hair coiled on her head with a bow holding it, her green Western-style dress exactly matching her eyes and showing off her beautiful figure.

"I wish things had worked out for you. Your job must be rough," Abby commiserated.

Shelby smiled back. "Oh, I like it," she said. "And at least we've got the house. We'll finish the last details of the sale next week, and then all the gossip will die down and we'll have our privacy back." She picked up her glass of ginger ale and sipped it. "I hope you don't mind my being a third wheel…."

"You go on," Abby replied. "You know Ty and I are just friends. I'm glad to have your company, and I'm sure your brother is, too."

Tyler smiled, but the look he sent her over Shelby's oblivious head wasn't quite platonic.

"Let's get in that next set," Tyler said, pulling Abby up by the hand. "Shelby, order Abby and me a ginger ale, would you?" he asked his sister.

She grinned. "Of course."

Abby stared at Tyler as he led her into the throng of dancers. "I can have a gin and tonic if I want to."

"Not while you're out with me," he said firmly, leading her into place in front of him. "I don't drink. That means you don't drink."

"Spoilsport," she sighed.

He chuckled. "Shame on you. You don't need booze to have a good time."

"I know. But I had looked forward to being treated like an adult," she told him.

"Well, don't give up hope," he said, his voice deep and soft as his lean hand curled around her waist. "The night's still young yet."

Abby smiled, because of course he was just flirting. She let him jostle her around the dance floor, graceful on his feet, expertly leading her through the twists and turns and shuffles and exchanges. Abby was having a great time until she glanced at the table where Justin and Calhoun were sitting. Justin's dark eyes kept darting over to Shelby. Abby was too far away to read his expression. Calhoun, on the other hand, was glaring at Abby and Tyler with enough venom for ten rattlesnakes.

Her heart leaped at the jealousy she saw on his face. Maybe there was still a little hope. The thought perked her up, and she began to smile, and then to laugh. Tyler mistook her response for pleasure in his company, and so did Calhoun. By the time the dance was over, Abby was caught in the middle of a building storm.

It threatened to explode when Calhoun, sick of watching Abby with Tyler, went and asked Shelby to dance.

Shelby was hesitant because Justin had just straightened at his table and looked capable of starting a world war all by himself.

"He won't mind," Calhoun said. "You look lonely sitting here by yourself."

"Oh, Calhoun, don't start anything," she pleaded.

"I won't," he promised. "Now come and dance with me."

Shelby gave in, but her lovely face was troubled.

Abby watched them go onto the dance floor, and her spirits fell. Shelby and Calhoun looked good together, her brunette beauty a perfect foil for his blond good looks. Abby felt plain and unattractive by comparison. She stared at Ty's chest, hopelessly depressed. What if Calhoun had come because of Shelby? What if he was courting her now? She felt sick.

"I feel like I'm sitting on a time bomb," Tyler mused as he watched Calhoun and Shelby and then got a look at Justin's face. "I don't know what Calhoun's up to, but Justin looks dangerous. Even if he hates my sister, he still seems to consider her his personal property. Would you look at that scowl?"

Abby saw Justin's expression and was ashamed of herself for wishing he would get out of his chair and beat the hell out of Calhoun. She flushed with embarrassment. "If Justin was dancing with another woman, how do you think Shelby would feel?" she asked, looking up at him.

He pursed his lips, his green eyes dancing as they searched her face. "I hadn't considered that."

"Calhoun probably thought Shelby was uncomfortable sitting by herself with nobody to dance with," Abby added.

Tyler sighed, his eyes wandering quietly over Abby's distracted expression as she looked toward the other couple on the floor. And all at once a lot of things became clear for him. Foremost was that Abby was jealous. Her eyes weren't any softer than Justin's. If she wasn't already in love with Calhoun, she was well on the way to it. Tyler felt all his chances slipping away, and there wasn't a thing he could do about it.

The evening wore on, and the tension rose. Calhoun seemed to enjoy dancing with Shelby. Abby stuck with Tyler. Justin sat and drank quietly by himself after he finished his business with the other gentleman, who left. The tall man began to look more coldly violent by the minute.

Toward the end of the dance, Calhoun left Shelby long enough to saunter over to Abby, who was sipping ginger ale while Tyler spoke to someone he knew at a nearby table. Abby hadn't been watching Calhoun, because he was making her miserable. He didn't smile at her anymore. He hated her, she was sure of it. So when

Calhoun appeared in front of her, Abby grew flustered and nervous and almost spilled her drink.

Calhoun saw the nervous motion, and it gave him hope. "How about dancing one with me?" he asked quietly.

She looked up, her eyes searching his face almost hungrily. "No, I'd better not," she said softly.

He caught his breath at the wounded sound in her voice. "Abby, why not?" he asked.

"It might hurt Shelby's feelings," she said, and turned away, searching the room desperately for Tyler. "I can't imagine where Tyler got to," she added huskily.

Calhoun looked like a radio with the transistors removed. He blinked, doubting that he'd really heard what she'd just said. Shelby might be hurt? Surely she didn't think—It suddenly dawned on him that if Abby was crazy enough to imagine he was getting involved with Shelby, Justin might, too.

He turned toward the table where Justin was sitting like a statue, and whistled under his breath. "Oh, my God," he breathed. "I've done it now."

Abby didn't say another word. She watched Calhoun move through the crowd toward Justin and wondered absently if his life insurance was paid up. Justin looked murderous.

There were two full ashtrays in front of Justin, and one half-empty whisky glass. The older man drank on occasion, but usually not when he was angry. If he did, he limited himself to one drink. The glass was what told Calhoun how angry his older brother was.

Calhoun sat down across from him, leaning back to study the older man. "She was lonely," he told Justin.

Justin drained his glass and rose, his eyes blacker

than Calhoun had seen them in a long time. "Then I'll see what I can do about it."

While Calhoun was catching his breath, Justin walked to Shelby's table. He didn't say a word. He looked at the woman until her face colored, then simply held out his hand. She put hers into it. He pulled her onto the dance floor, and they melted into each other to a slow, dreamy tune.

Abby sighed as she watched them. They were stiff, as if there were more than just space between them, but the look on Shelby's face was hauntingly beautiful. His expression was less easily read, hard and rigid. But Abby would have bet that he was as close to heaven as he'd been in six years.

"How about that for a surprise?" Tyler murmured over her head, watching. "My God, look at them. They're like two halves of a whole."

"Why did they ever split up?" she asked him.

"I don't know," he said with a sigh. "I think my father was mixed up in it somehow, and one of his friends. But Shelby never talks about it. All I know is that she gave him back his ring and he's been bitter ever since."

As the music ended, the couple stopped dancing. Justin released Shelby very slowly and abruptly turned and walked out of the dance hall. After a minute, Shelby went back and sat down. Calhoun returned to the table.

Abby, turning to watch Calhoun bend toward Shelby, felt even sicker when she saw Shelby get up and leave the building, holding Calhoun's arm.

She toughed it out for several more dances, but when Calhoun didn't come back, she finally realized that he'd more than likely taken Shelby home. And was still there...

"Can we go home, Ty?" she asked huskily.

"Are you sure that's what you want?" Ty asked, his voice full of sympathy.

"I'm tired," Abby replied, and it was no lie. She really was. She was tired of watching Calhoun in action. First the blonde, now Shelby, and all in one week. But plain little Abby didn't figure in his world. She didn't even matter. She looked up at Ty, her eyes misty with unshed tears. "Do you mind?"

"Of course I mind," he said gently. "But if that's what you want, we'll go."

Abby didn't speak all the way home. It was unlike Calhoun to deliberately start trouble. It was almost as if he were getting back at Justin for something, but for what? Justin hadn't done anything to him.

Tyler walked her up the steps onto the long front porch with its graceful arches and porch furniture.

"Sorry the evening ended so abruptly," Tyler said. "But I hope you had fun."

"I did, honestly," she said, smiling up at him.

He took a deep breath and bent toward her hesitantly. When she didn't resist, he brushed his mouth gently against hers. There was no response, and after a minute he lifted his dark head.

His green eyes searched hers, and he wasn't smiling. "You don't have a clue, do you, honey?" he asked gently. "And I think it's lack of interest more than just lack of experience."

"You think I'm green as grass, too, I guess," she sighed miserably.

He cocked an eyebrow and tweaked her chin with his lean fingers. "So that's how it is." He pursed his lips. "Well, little Abby, with some cooperation from you I could take care of the green part in about five minutes.

But I think that's a lesson the man you're mooning over should teach you." He touched his lips to her forehead. "I hope he appreciates his good luck. You're a special girl."

"He doesn't think so, but I'm glad you do." She looked up at him with a faint smile. "I wish it could be you."

His expression hardened for just an instant before the old mocking humor came back. "So do I. Want to go to dinner one night? Just a friendly dinner. I know when a door's being closed, so you won't have any worries on that score."

Her smile grew brighter. "You're a nice man."

"Not always." He touched her cheek gently. "Good night."

"Good night, Tyler. I had a good time."

"So did I."

He took the steps two at a time, and Abby stood quietly, watching him drive off. It was a long time before she turned and went into the house.

She closed the front door and started toward the staircase, only to be stopped in her tracks by an off-key rendition of a Mexican drinking song. Somewhere in the back of her mind she recognized it as one Justin sang on the very rare occasions when he had had too many glasses of whiskey.

Chapter 7

Abby went all the way inside the house and closed the door. Then she slipped down the hall to the study and peeked in.

Justin was holding a square whiskey glass. It was empty. He was sprawled on the leather sofa with his dark hair in his eyes and his shirt rumpled, one big boot propped on the spotless leather seat, singing for all he was worth. On the coffee table beside him were a smokeless ashtray, a crumpled cigarette pack, a fresh cigarette pack, and half a bottle of whiskey.

"No puedo hacer..." He stopped at the sound of her footsteps and looked up at her with bloodshot eyes.

"Oh, Justin," she moaned.

"Hello, Abby. Want a snort?"

She grimaced at the glass he held up. "It's empty," she told him.

He stared at it. "Damn. I guess it is. Well, I'll fill it up, then."

He threw his leg off the sofa, almost ending up on the floor in the process.

Abby put down her purse and coat and helped him onto the sofa. "Justin, this won't help," she said. "You know it won't."

"She cried," Justin murmured. "Damn it, she cried. And he took her home. I want to kill him, Abby," he said, his eyes blazing, his voice harsh. "My own brother, and I want to kill him because he went off with her!"

She bit her lower lip. She didn't know what to say, what to do. Justin never drank, and he never complained. But he looked as if he were dying, and Abby could sympathize. She'd felt that way, too, when Calhoun had left with Shelby.

"I saw them go," he ground out. He put his face in his lean hands and sighed heavily. "She's part of me. Still part of me after all the years, all the pain. Calhoun knew it, Abby, he did it deliberately…."

"Calhoun loves you," she defended him. "He wouldn't hurt you on purpose."

"Any man could fall in love with her," he kept on. "Shelby's beautiful. A dream walking."

Abby knew how attractive Shelby was. The knowledge didn't help her own sense of failure, her own lack of confidence or her breaking heart.

"Drinking isn't the answer," she said softly. She touched his arm. "Justin, get some sleep."

"How can I sleep when he's with her?"

"He won't be for long. Tyler just went home," she said tautly.

He took a deep breath, letting it out in jerks. His hands came away from his eyes. "I don't know much about women, Abby," he said absently. "I don't have Calhoun's charm, or his experience, or his looks."

She felt a sense of kinship with him then, because she had the same problem. Justin had always seemed so self-assured that she'd never thought of him having the same doubts and fears that she did.

"And I don't have Shelby's assets," Abby confessed. She sat down beside him. "I guess we'd both lose a beauty contest. I wish I was blond, Justin."

"I wish I had a black book." Justin sighed.

She grinned at him, and he grinned back. He poured whiskey into the glass, getting half again as much on the heavy coffee table. "Here," he offered it to her. "To hell with both of them. Have a shot of ego salve."

"Thanks, masked man," she sighed, taking it. "Don't mind if I do."

It tasted horrible. "Can you really drink this stuff and live?" she wondered. "It smells like what you put in the gas tank."

"It's Scotch whiskey," he returned. "Cutty Sark."

"It would cutty a shark all right," she mused, sipping it.

"Not cutty a shark. Cutty Shark. Sark. Hell." He took the glass and finished what little whiskey she'd left. "Now, if you're going to drink Cutty Sark, Abby, you have to learn to sing properly. I'll teach you this song I learned down in Mexico, okay?"

And he proceeded to do just that. When Calhoun walked in the front door about thirty minutes later, there was a very loud off-key chorus coming from the study.

He stared in the door incredulously. Justin was lying back on the sofa, his hair in his eyes, one knee lifted, a whiskey bottle in his hand. Abby was lying against his uplifted knee, her legs thrown over the coffee table, sipping from a whiskey glass. She looked as disreputable as his brother did, and both of them looked soaked to the back teeth.

"What in hell is going on?" Calhoun asked as he leaned against the doorjamb.

"We hate you," Abby informed him, lifting her glass in a toast.

"Amen." Justin grinned.

"And just as soon as we get through drinking and singing, we're going to go down to the feedlot and open all the gates, and you can spend the rest of the night chasing cows." She smiled drunkenly. "Justin and I figure that's what you do best, anyway. Chasing females, that is. So it doesn't matter what species, does it, old buddy?" she asked Justin, twisting her head back against his knee.

"Nope," Justin agreed. He lifted the whiskey bottle to his lips, rolling backward a little as he sipped it.

"We were going to lock you out," Abby added, blinking, "but we couldn't get up to put on the chain latches."

"My God." Calhoun shook his head at the spectacle they made. "I wish I had a camera."

"What for?" Justin asked pleasantly.

"Never mind." Calhoun unbuttoned his cuffs and rolled up his sleeves. "I'll make some black coffee."

"Don't want any," Abby murmured drowsily. "It would mess up our systems."

"That's right," Justin agreed.

"You'll see messed-up systems by morning, all right." Calhoun grimaced and moved off toward the kitchen.

"We should check his collar for lipstick!" Abby told Justin in a stage whisper.

"Good idea," Justin frowned. He started to sit up, then fell back against the arm of the sofa, cradling the bottle. "In a minute. I have to rest first."

"That's okay," she said. "I'll do it." She yawned. "When he gets back." Her eyes closed.

By the time Calhoun got back, they were both snoring. The whiskey bottle was lying on the floor, with the neck in Justin's lean hand. Calhoun righted it and put it on the table along with Abby's empty glass. The sight of them was as puzzling as it was amusing. Both Justin and Abby were usually the teetotalers at any gathering, and here they were soused. He wondered if his leaving with Shelby had set them off and realized that it probably had. In Justin's case it was understandable. But Abby's state was less easily understood, after the way she'd treated him since he'd kissed her. Unless…

He frowned, his dark eyes quiet and curious as he watched her flushed, sleeping face. Unless she'd finally realized why he'd been rough with her and was regretting her hot words. Was that possible? She'd seemed jealous of the time he'd spent with Shelby at the dance, and here she was three sheets to the wind. Well, well. Miracles did happen, it seemed.

He still wasn't sure about Tyler Jacobs's feelings toward Abby, but at least now he didn't have to worry about Justin's. If just seeing his brother with Shelby had this effect on Justin, he was still crazy about Shelby.

Calhoun lifted Abby and sat her crookedly in a chair while he laid Justin down on the sofa, pulled the older man's big boots off and covered him with one of the colorful serapes that were draped on chairs all over the room. Then he swung Abby up in his arms, balanced her on his knee while he turned off the overhead light, and closed the study door. Justin was going to hate himself in the morning.

Abby stirred as he carried her up the staircase. Her eyes flickered open, and she stared up drunkenly at the hard, quiet face above hers.

"You're with Shelby," she muttered drowsily. "We know you are. We know what you're doing, too." She laughed bitterly, then sighed and broke into the Mexican song Justin had taught her.

"Stop that." Calhoun scowled at her. "My God, you shouldn't use language like that."

"What language?"

"That song Justin taught you," he muttered, topping the staircase and heading down the hall toward her room. "It's vulgar as all hell."

"He didn't say it was."

"Of course he didn't. He wouldn't have taught it to you if he'd been sober. He'll have a heart attack if he hears you singing it when he's back on his feet."

"Want me to teach it to you?" she asked.

"I already know it."

"That isn't surprising," she sighed. She closed her eyes as he walked through the open door into her room and kicked it shut behind him. There were memories in this room, he thought angrily as he headed toward the bed. Abby, half-naked on that pink coverlet. Abby's soft body under his against that far wall—where she'd put a bookcase. He frowned at it. The new furniture arrangement was fairly revealing. Why would she shift the bookcase there unless it bothered her to remember?

He laid her down on the bed and watched her curl up. "No, you don't," he murmured. "You can't go to sleep like that."

She yawned. "Yes, I can."

He pulled off her shoes, and after a moment's hesitation his hard fingers went to her skirt. He removed it and about a hundred layers of full underskirts, and then her panty hose and blouse. Under it all, she was wearing dainty pink lace briefs and a matching bra that was no cover at all over her full, firm breasts.

This, he thought as he looked at her, was a hell of a mistake. But she was the most delicious little morsel. Her body was perfect, the most beautiful he'd seen in his life. And when he realized just how innocent she was, how untouched, his body rippled with pleasure mingled with need.

She sighed then, and her eyes opened. She searched his face, watching where his gaze had fallen. "You undressed me," she said.

"You couldn't sleep in that rig," he replied tautly.

"I guess not." She knew it should bother her that he was seeing her like this, in those wispy pink things she'd been crazy enough to buy at Misty's insistence. But if the way he was staring at her was any indication, he seemed to like what he saw.

"Do you have pajamas or a gown?" he asked after a minute.

"A gown. Under my pillow."

He managed to make his legs move and took out a bit of material that would cover no more of her than her underwear. "You'll freeze to death in this thing," he muttered.

"Misty said it was a sexy outfit," she said drowsily. She moved, her long hair framing her oval face with its delicate flush, her pale blue-gray eyes enormous as they searched the faintly blurred outline of his body. "I thought I'd seduce Ty," she added. "He likes me."

His face hardened. "Like hell you will," he said shortly.

"You did that to Shelby," she accused. "Shame on you, when Justin loves her."

"I didn't touch Shelby," he returned. "I left her at her front door and went back to the dance hall looking for you."

"I wasn't there," she murmured.

"Obviously." He didn't mention that he'd had to fight the urge to go looking for Tyler's car in case he and Abby were parked somewhere. The thought of her with Ty made him want to do something violent.

"Justin is going to beat you up when he can stand up again," she told him gaily.

"I guess he's entitled." Calhoun sighed. "I sure as hell made a mess of things." He sat down beside her, his eyes reluctantly leaving the long, sweet line of her legs and hips and the open seductiveness of her almost-bare breasts. "Do you know how perfect you are?" he said absently.

She was suddenly cold sober. Her eyes opened wide, searching his. "Me?"

"You," he said harshly. "From your legs to your hips to those sweet, pretty brea—" He stopped, hating his own vulnerability. "Come here." He put the gown in her lap and drew her into a sitting position, watching the tips of her firm breasts suddenly harden. He caught his breath.

She looked up at him curiously. "What's wrong?"

"This." He touched her delicately, only the back of his knuckles rubbing softly against her nipples. She pulled away, her breath audible, and he lifted his head to search her shocked eyes.

She looked back at him, relaxed from the alcohol,

all her deeply buried longings surfacing without the restraint of a usually protective mind. She touched the back of his hand and intertwined her fingers with his. And then she pulled gently, watching as she drew his hand across her breasts.

"Abby..." he ground out.

"I'm sorry, " she whispered. "About what I said that morning. About how I...reacted." She swallowed, searching for courage. She opened his fingers and pressed them hesitantly just underneath her breast, lifting them so that he could feel the swell against his skin.

"Don't, for God's sake," he groaned.

She moved his hand against her, drowning in the sweetness of his touch, arching toward it. Both her hands went there, pushing his fingers completely over her. "Calhoun," she moaned. She felt so weak that she thought she'd have to lie down again, but she couldn't let go of his hand.

"You aren't sober enough," he whispered roughly, although the feel of her was doing terrible things to his self-control. He was already going rigid with need as he followed her down.

"I'm not sober enough to be afraid," she whispered. Her eyes searched his glittering eyes. "Teach me."

He actually shuddered. "I can't."

"Why?" she asked. "Because I'm plain and unsophisticated, because I'm not blond—" Her voice broke.

So did his control. He leaned down, his smoky breath mingling with hers as his hand cupped her. "Because you're a virgin," he breathed into her mouth as he took it.

She moaned. It was sweet, so sweet. Nothing like

that other time, when he'd been rough and hadn't given her enough room to respond. He'd been impatient and demanding, but now he was gentle. His fingers stroked her body from her breasts to her waist to her flat stomach. His mouth teased at hers, probed it, traced it in a silence that was thick with sensual pleasure. Abby felt warm all over, safe and cared-about. She let her lips admit the probing of his tongue, admit him into the sweet darkness of her mouth. She didn't even protest when the kiss grew much deeper, much slower, or when she felt his hand slide under her to find the catch at her back.

The air was cool on her body. He removed the lacy covering that was no covering at all, and his hands were heaven on her hot skin. She moaned, helping him, pressing his fingers against her, drawing them over her hungry body.

"Abby," he groaned against her mouth, half-crazy with the hunger to make love to her completely, to salve the ache that was throbbing through his body.

She opened her eyes, letting her gaze fall lazily to his chest. Her hands went to his shirt, and she worked at the buttons, feeling him tense. But he didn't protest, even though his heartbeat was shaking his big body as it lay beside hers.

"There," she whispered when she could see and touch the thick wedge of hair that ran down to his belt. "I'll bet women love to touch you there," she murmured as she pressed her fingers hungrily against him.

"I've never let a woman touch me like this before," he said huskily. "I didn't like it until now."

Her eyes searched his, and she shifted restlessly on the coverlet, hungry, aching for something without a name, without an image.

"What do you want?" he asked gruffly, searching her eyes. "Tell me. I'll do anything you want me to."

She swallowed, and her lips parted unsteadily. She took his head in her hands and tugged at it, lifting her body. And he understood without her having to put it into words.

"Here?" he whispered tenderly, and put his open mouth completely over the swollen tip of her breast.

She moaned helplessly. It was beyond her wildest imaginings of what passion would feel like. Her body was in control. Her mind could only watch, it couldn't slow down what was happening. She twisted the cool, thick strands of his blond hair while he smoothed his warm mouth over her breasts and stomach, her faint cries encouraging him, her body welcoming him.

His mouth slid back up to meet hers. And as she opened her own lips to welcome him, she felt his body slowly cover her.

Her eyes opened then as his mouth lifted fractionally, and she watched his face, hard with passion, as his body fit itself perfectly to her slenderness.

She barely breathed, her eyes wide and full of new knowledge as she felt him intimately and knew without words how badly he wanted her.

"Are you afraid this time?" he whispered quietly.

"I should be," she replied. She reached up and touched his face as he drew his chest slowly, teasingly over her breasts. Her breath caught, but she traced his eyebrows, his cheeks, his mouth with fingers that trembled and adored him.

His big, calloused hands slid under her back, lifting her up into the curve of his body. "I want you, Abby," he whispered, bending to her mouth as his body shuddered over hers. "I want you so much…."

She curled her arms around his head and held his mouth against her eager one. "I want you, too, Calhoun," she whispered into his mouth.

He almost lost control completely then. He kissed her until he had to stop for breath, his body shuddering rhythmically, his knee between her long, soft legs, his hand low on her hips. He felt her trembling and heard her whimper. Oddly, it brought him to his senses.

Slowly, so slowly, he rolled onto his side, bringing her with him, cradling her against his damp body. He slid his hands to her head, holding her forehead to his throbbing chest.

"Lie still, honey," he whispered raggedly when she began to move again. He caught her hips and stilled them. "Just lie against me and breathe. It will be all right in a minute. Lie still, baby."

Her hands were flat against his chest, trembling there in the thick mat of hair, and she felt his unsteady breathing against her hair. He was as shaken as she was, but why had he stopped? She didn't understand. If he wanted her, then why had he stopped?

"Sweet thing," he breathed when the tremor was almost out of his big arms. "Sweet, precious thing, another few seconds and nothing on earth would have stopped me, did you know?"

She nuzzled her head against him. "Why did you stop?" she asked dazedly.

He tilted her head back on the pillow and smiled into her drowsy eyes. "Don't you know?"

"Because I'm not blond, I guess," she sighed, almost weeping with frustration and disappointment.

"Because you're not lucid," he corrected. He brushed the long, soft hair away from her face. "Abby, you're half lit."

"I want you," she moaned.

"I know. I can see it. Feel it." He hugged her close for a minute, because he was almost in control now. Then he let go and quickly and efficiently slid her into her gown. "Sit up, honey."

She did, and he eased back the covers and helped her get under them. She lay quietly beneath two layers of fabric and blinked at him sleepily. "Calhoun, stay with me," she whispered.

He smiled gently, his dark eyes possessive on her flushed face. "Justin would love finding us in your bed together. He'd probably make me marry you."

"And I guess that would be the end of your world," she replied.

His expression hardened. He drew in a slow breath and touched her cheek gently, thoughtfully. "I've been alone a long time. I like being my own boss, answering to no one. I've been a rounder, and in some ways I still am. I'm a bad marriage risk."

"One woman wouldn't satisfy you, I guess," she murmured, hiding her eyes from him. All her dreams were dead now. Every last one. He wanted her, but not enough for marriage. He was telling her so.

He shrugged, confused and feeling faintly hunted. "One woman never has," he said curtly. "I don't want to be tied."

"God forbid that I should try," Abby said, forcing a smile. "Don't worry, Calhoun, I was just...experimenting. I wondered why you were so rough with me the other morning, and I wanted to see if passion made people rough. I guess it does, because that's how I felt tonight. Thanks for the...the lesson."

He frowned slightly, searching her eyes. "Is that all it felt like. An experiment? A lesson in making love?"

"Tyler said I needed teaching," she said with a yawn, missing the flash of fury in his face. "But I don't anymore." She closed her eyes and turned her face against the pillow. "I'm sleepy."

Calhoun sat watching her, his eyes stormy. She'd used him. That was all she'd wanted. She'd been experimenting, seeing how it felt to be touched. Damn her!

He got up, glaring at the lacy bra he'd removed from her soft breasts just before she'd let him touch them. Let him! God, she'd helped him! His blood ran hot at the memory of how uninhibited she'd been with him tonight. Had she been competing with Shelby, or had it been curiosity alone? Could she care about him and be hiding it? And how did he feel? Did he just want her physically, or was it more than that? Could he bear the loss of his freedom? Because it would come to that if he took her. Marriage. Trap.

He tossed the bra onto the chair beside her bed and took a long last look at her sleeping face. She didn't need to be blond. She was exquisite. Her long hair was spread out around her, her lashes were feathering her flushed cheek, and her parted lips were pink and faintly swollen because he'd been hungry. She was delicious. Virginal and sweet-tasting and exquisitely beautiful without her clothes. He wondered if he'd ever get over the taste of her—if he'd be able to forget. Hell, would he ever be able to have another woman, or would the memory of Abby always stand in the way?

He opened the door and went out, closing it quietly behind him. He should never have touched her in the first place, he thought furiously.

He had to get away for a while. Far away, so that he could think things through. Now that he'd touched

Abby, it was going to be the purest kind of hell keeping his hands off her. And Justin wouldn't like having that sort of loveplay going on, not if it threatened Abby. Calhoun knew that if he took Abby into his arms again, it wasn't going to end with a few kisses. He wanted her too badly, and she was too responsive. He aroused her as no man ever had. That meant she'd give herself to him with hardly any coaxing. Calhoun was terrified that he might lose his head and take her.

He didn't want marriage. He didn't want ties. Abby wouldn't understand that. In her world, lovemaking meant marriage. Maybe in his, too, when the woman was a virgin. He didn't like the noose she was tying around his neck, but he hated the thought of never touching her again almost as much.

She was heaven to love. Her mouth was young and sweet and so eager to learn. Her body was nectar. Just the sight of it made him drunk, not to mention the exquisite feel of it between his hands, under his skin.

Abby, he groaned inwardly as he made his way to his own room. He couldn't have her and he couldn't give her up. He didn't know what in hell he was going to do. Maybe when he got back from wherever he wound up he would have reached a decision.

He sat down at the small desk in a corner of his room and wrote Justin a note telling him he was going away for a few days to check on some stockers in Montana. Justin might think it strange, but Abby wouldn't. He wondered how she was going to feel when she woke up and found him gone. He hoped she wouldn't even remember what they'd done in her bed together. But even if she did, that was going to be one private memory. Abby wouldn't share it any more than he would.

Chapter 8

Abby groaned the minute the light got to her eyes. She had the world's biggest headache, and nausea sat in the pit of her stomach like acid.

She managed to get on her feet and into the bathroom, where she bathed her face with cold water and pressed a cold cloth against her eyes. She remembered drinking whiskey in the study with Justin. Then Calhoun had taken her to bed, and—

Her head jerked up. In the mirror her eyes looked wild, and her paleness had been eclipsed by a scarlet blush. She'd let Calhoun see her. Worse, she'd let him touch her. She swallowed. Well, at least she remembered that he'd stopped before she'd gone to sleep, so nothing unspeakable had happened, thank God. As more of the details of her eagerness came back, she groaned in embarrassment. She'd never be able to look at him again, although what had happened would make the sweetest of memories to tuck in a corner of her mind for solace in her old age. Calhoun would never settle down or fall in love with her. He'd be forever out chasing his blondes. But this was something of him that Abby would always have. A tiny crumb of loving to live on.

Now she understood what had happened that morning in her room. He hadn't been rough on purpose. He'd wanted her. It gave her the oddest feeling of pride that she could have thrown him that far off balance. She was almost sure that no other woman ever had. Looking back, she thought she must have seemed terribly naive to him for reacting that way to an intimate kiss. But at the time his actions had seemed shocking and frightening. For all her dreams about Calhoun, she hadn't realized what the reality of his lovemaking would be like. Now that she knew, it was like an addiction. She wanted more. But could she afford the risk of letting him that close again?

A sob racked her slender body. Well, she had to get herself together. She had to remember her pride. She held her aching head. She had to remember, most of all, to never accept a drink of whiskey from Justin again! Or from anyone, for that matter. Drowning one's sorrows was vastly overrated. She'd tried it, and now she knew that it only brought hangovers, not oblivion.

She put on a gray slacks suit with a blue blouse, left her hair around her shoulders because she was hurting too much to worry with putting it up, and pulled on a pair of sunglasses. Then she felt her way down the staircase and into the dining room.

Justin was sitting at the table with his head in his hands. He was dressed in jeans and a blue checked shirt, and when he looked up, his eyes looked even worse than Abby's.

"Nice touch," he remarked, noticing the dark glasses. "I wish I had mine, but they're out in the car."

"You look like I feel," Abby said as she sat down, very gently, in the chair beside him, grimacing because even that slight jarring made her head feel like bursting. "How are we going to work today?"

"Beats me," Justin replied. "Calhoun's gone."

Her heart skipped a beat, and she was glad she was wearing dark glasses. "Is he?"

"Skipped town. Gone to Montana to look at stockers, or so he said." He fumbled for a cigarette and lit it. "I'm rather disappointed. I had consoled myself all morning with the thought of beating the hell out of him for last night."

"How selfish," Abby muttered as she tried to pour herself a cup of hot coffee from the carafe. "I ought to get in a lick or two of my own."

"I'll sit on him, you can hit him," Justin offered. He sipped black coffee and smoked quietly.

Abby took one swallow of her coffee and sat back, feeling miserable. "Weren't we singing something?" she thought, frowning. "Oh, yes, I remember…." She launched into a few measures of the song. Justin went white, and Maria came running out of the kitchen, beet red, waving her apron.

A tidal wave of Spanish hit Abby between the eyes, delivered in a scolding, furious tone. "For shame, for shame!" Maria wound up breathlessly, crossing herself. "Where you learn such terrible language?"

Abby stared at her blankly. "Justin taught me," she said.

Justin had his face in his hands. Maria launched into him, and he replied in the same tongue, a little sheepishly. Maria shook her head and stormed out of the room.

"What did I say?" Abby asked him, wide-eyed.

He took a slow breath. "You don't want to know," he said finally. "I think you'd better forget the song, Abby, or we're going to be eating burned meals for a month."

"You taught it to me," she pointed out.

He groaned. "I was sauced. That was a drinking song I learned when I was barely out of school from one of the Mexican boys I used to pal around with. I didn't even remember it until last night, and I never should have taught it to you."

"It's all Calhoun's fault," she said.

"I wonder why he started it?" Justin asked, watching her. "He didn't show any signs of wanting to dance until he saw you and Tyler."

Abby shifted restlessly in her chair. "Well, he doesn't want me," she said miserably. "Not on any permanent basis, anyway. He told me last night that he was a bad marriage risk. He likes variety, you see."

"Most men do, until they find themselves so hopelessly enthralled with one woman that they can't even look at anyone else," Justin said tersely, staring at his coffee.

"Is that why you spend all your time alone?" she asked gently, searching his hard, drawn face. "Because your world begins and ends with Shelby?"

He glared at her. "Abby…"

"Sorry." She sipped the coffee. "It's just that I know how it feels now." She traced the pattern of her lipstick on the edge of the cup. "I feel that way about your stupid, blind brother."

The brief anger left his face, and he smiled gently. "I

could pretend to be surprised, but I'm not. You're pretty obvious. On the other hand," he added, tilting his head back, "so is he. In all the years Calhoun's been dating, this is the first time I've ever seen him behave as if he were jealous."

Abby bit her lower lip. "He…wants me," she said. She couldn't look at him as she said it.

"Of course," he replied carelessly, smiling at her shocked expression. "Abby, for a man that's a big part of caring about a woman."

"I guess I don't know very much about men," she said with a sigh. "In fact, I don't know anything. Except that I want to live with him all my life, and have children with him, and look after him when he's sick, and keep him company when he's lonely." She bit her lower lip. "So, that being the case, Justin, I think I'd better get out while I still can. Before something happens and Calhoun winds up trapped." She looked up at Justin, her fear plain in her eyes. "You understand, don't you?"

He nodded. "I think you're very wise, Abby. If he cares enough, he'll come after you. If he doesn't…you might save both of you a lot of heartache by heading off trouble." He shrugged. "But I'll miss having you around."

"I'll come back and visit." She sipped more coffee, and as she began to feel a little better she took off her dark glasses. "Can I still have my twenty-first birthday party here?"

"Sure," he said readily.

"You may not approve of my guest list," she added gently.

He took a deep breath. "Tyler Jacobs will be on it, I gather."

"And Shelby." He glared at her, and she smiled

hesitantly. "Justin, I can't very well invite him and not her. How would it look?"

"Calhoun might—" He stopped short.

Abby lifted her chin. "I have to stop caring what Calhoun does, and so do you. And if you don't like Calhoun paying attention to Shelby, why not do something about it?" she added impishly. "You might get her drunk and teach her that terrible song."

He almost smiled. "I did once," he said, his dark eyes softening at the memory. "The night we got engaged." Then he flinched and got up from the table. "I've got to try and go to work. How about you? Can you make it?"

"Of course I can." She stood up, feeling as wobbly as he looked. She glanced at him ruefully. "Shall we flip a coin and see who drives?"

He chuckled. "I think I'd better. I've got more practice at it than you have. Come on."

They muddled through the day, and at the end of it Abby called Mrs. Simpson and asked if she could go ahead and move in later that week. The older woman was delighted and promised to have the room ready. Then, with a heavy heart, Abby began to pack up her things, getting ready to say goodbye to the only home she'd known for the past five and a half years. Worst of all was the realization that once she left it she'd probably never see Calhoun again. Although she hadn't mentioned it to Justin yet, she'd decided to quit her job at the feedlot, too. The prospect of seeing Calhoun every day, knowing that he wanted her but had no love for her, would tear her heart out.

Justin and two of the cowhands helped her get her possessions over to Mrs. Simpson's house. Since the room was furnished, she hadn't tried to take furniture with her, but she had plenty of clothes and records and books to carry. Her stereo and her color television went with her, along with her memorabilia. It was easier to think about living elsewhere with her belongings around. But after having a home of her own, even if she had shared it with the brothers, it was hard to adjust to a small apartment in someone else's house.

She gave notice at the feedlot the very next day. It was hard, but Justin seemed to understand. He didn't say a word. He just smiled.

But Calhoun didn't understand. He came back unexpectedly in the middle of the following week, and when Abby came back from lunch it was to find him sitting on the corner of her desk, looking worn and smoking like a furnace.

She stared at him with eyes that adored him. It had only been a few days. A little over a week. But she'd ached for him. To be without him was like having part of her body cut away, and she didn't know how she was going to manage to hide her feelings from him.

He was wearing a beige suit with a striped shirt, and his blond hair gleamed clean and thick in the light from the office window. He scowled over his cigarette.

She straightened the skirt of her pale blue dress nervously, waiting for him to look up. Then he did, and she saw the darkness of his eyes, the faint shadows under them.

He looked at her for a long time, oblivious to the noise around them, the ringing telephones, the buzz of printers. He looked at her until she felt uncomfortably warm and she blushed.

"You've moved out," he said without preamble.

"Yes," she replied huskily.

"And you've put in your notice here."

She took a deep breath, moving a little closer. He smelled of spice and soap, and she stared unconsciously at his mouth, remembering its exquisite sweetness on her lips. "I...I'm going to work for George Brady and his father," she said. "At the insurance office. I'm used to working with forms, so it won't be so unfamiliar."

"Why?" he ground out.

She smoothed her lower lip with her tongue, looking up at him with soft, wounded eyes.

"Here," he muttered, catching her arm. He pulled her into his office and closed the door behind them, frowning down at her. He didn't let go even then. His fingers were warm and firm through her soft sleeve, and their touch made her tingle.

"You know I can't stay in the house anymore," she whispered. "You know why."

"Are you that afraid of me?" he asked quietly.

She shifted restlessly, letting her eyes slide down to his firm jaw. "I'm afraid of what could happen."

"I see."

It was embarrassing to talk to him about it, but he had to know how vulnerable she was. It wasn't anything he hadn't guessed. She studied his patterned red tie carelessly.

"I suppose I sound conceited," she added. "But... but if you—" Her eyes closed. "I'm vulnerable," she whispered. Her lower lip trembled, and she bit it. "Oh, Calhoun, I'm so vulnerable—"

"Don't you think I know?" he said under his breath, and the eyes that met hers were dark with emotion. "Why do you think I left?"

She couldn't look at him anymore. She felt naked. "Well, I'm saving you from any more complications," she said tightly. "I won't be around."

He couldn't seem to breathe. His cigarette had burned out, and it hung in his hand, as dead as he felt. "Is that what you want?"

She straightened. "Tyler's taking me to dinner tonight," she said out of the blue, just to let him see that she wasn't going to try to hang on to him or act lovesick. "He's got a job, too, by the way. He's going to manage old man Regan's ranch for him. In no time at all he'll be settled and able to take on more responsibilities."

Calhoun's heart felt like lead in his chest. Was she saying what he thought she was? Was she implying that she might marry Tyler?

"You don't love him," he said harshly.

She looked up. "I don't need to," she replied quietly. "Love isn't anything. It's just an emotion that blinds people to reality."

"Abby!" he burst out. "You can't believe that?"

"Look who's talking." She glared at him. "You're the one who said it was for the birds, aren't you? You've never let your emotions get in the way of a good time!"

He took a slow, steadying breath, and his dark eyes searched hers in the static silence that followed. "Maybe that was true a few years ago," he admitted, his voice deep and slow and measured. "I've never had any trouble attracting women, and I had a sizable appetite back then. But I learned that sex by itself has very little flavor, and it didn't take long to realize that most of those women were trading their bodies for what I could give them." He laughed bitterly. "How would that appeal to you, tidbit? Being traded a few kisses and a night in bed for a car or a coat or some expensive jewelry, so that you never could be sure that it was you or your wallet they really wanted?"

She'd never heard him talk like this. He never had, at least not to her. She searched his face, finding cynicism and faint mockery in his smile, in his hard eyes.

"You're very attractive," she replied. "Surely you know that."

His big shoulders rose and fell. "Plenty of men are," he said without conceit. "But I'm rich with it. My money has appeal."

"Only to a certain type of woman," she reminded him. "One who doesn't want ties or emotional liabilities. One with mercenary tendencies who could walk away from you if you lost everything, or if you were sick or old." She smiled gently. "I suppose you liked that, too. You could be independent and still enjoy yourself."

He frowned a little, watching her. "I haven't had a woman since the night you went to the strip show," he said quietly.

She didn't want to hear about his love life. She turned her head. "You had dates…."

"Well, my God, I can date women without seducing them!"

"It's none of my business." She started to reach for the doorknob, but his big, warm hand engulfed hers, sensuously caressing her fingers as he moved closer, drowning her in the clean cologne-rich scent of him.

"Make it your business," he said tautly.

She looked up at him slowly, searchingly. But there was nothing readable in his face or his eyes or even the set of his head. It was like trying to learn from stone. "I don't understand," she said, her voice faltering.

"I don't like bridles," he said shortly. "I don't like the thought of ropes around me, or a ring through my nose. I hate the thought of marriage." He grimaced, but his eyes held hers. "But you're in my blood," he breathed. "And I don't know what to do about it."

"I won't sleep with you," she said with quiet pride. "And yes, I want to." She laughed bitterly. "More than I want to breathe."

"Yes. I knew that when I left." He touched her hair, smoothing it, tracing its length down to her shoulder with a possessive touch that made her tremble. "I know all too well how you feel about me. I suspected it the night you went to that bar with Misty and you whispered that you wished you were blond...." His dark eyes lanced up to her shocked ones. "And the night of the square dance cinched it. I did a lot of thinking while I was away. I managed to put two and two together at last."

She felt as if he'd cut the ground from under her feet. Stark naked. She'd thought her secret was safe, and now it wasn't.

"You don't need to deny it," he added when he saw her expression. "There's no reason to. I'm not going to make fun of you or try to embarrass you. But I told you the night I left how I felt. I'm twelve years older than you. I'm a rounder, and I haven't ever tried abstinence. You're even my ward. If I had any sense I'd let you go and wave you off, laughing. You're a complication I don't want or need."

"Thanks," she said shortly. Her face was flaming. It was embarrassing to have him see right through her, when she hadn't realized how transparent she must be to an experienced man.

"That's what my mind is telling me," he added, laughing with faint mockery as he moved closer. "Now let me show you what my body says—"

She opened her mouth to protest, but his lips covered hers before she could speak. His kiss was warm and slow, and when his hands went to her hips and pulled them against his and he let her feel the blatant hunger of his body, she gave in.

"So soft," he whispered as he brushed his lips over her mouth. "So sweet. I dream about kissing you. I dream about your body and the way you are with me when I make love to you. I want you more than I've ever wanted a woman in my life."

"That's...physical," she protested.

"That's all I can offer you," he replied. His lips moved to her eyelids, closing them with kisses. "Now do you see, Abby? I've never loved anyone. I've never wanted that. All you can have of me is this."

She swallowed. What a bitter, hopeless relationship that would be. She loved him with all her heart, and all he had to offer her was his body.

He tasted the tears before he saw them. His blond head lifted, and he winced at the sight of her drenched blue-gray eyes. "Oh, God, don't," he breathed, wiping the wetness away with his thumbs.

"Let me go, please," she pleaded, pushing at his broad, hard chest.

"You want something I can't give you."

"I know that now," she whispered. She bit on her lower lip to stop it from trembling, and stared at his tie. "I guess I was never cut out to be a mercenary blonde," she said with an attempt at humor, feeling his body stiffen as she made the remark. She looked up then, with drenched eyes that couldn't hide her hunger for his heart. "But I would have loved you so—"

"Abby," he groaned. His mouth silenced her, ardently, roughly. He wrapped her up in his hard arms, kissing her with such force that her head bent back against his arms, and still he didn't stop, couldn't stop. He began to tremble faintly, the hunger a living thing in him, torturously sweet.

But Abby couldn't bear the bitter mockery of a kiss that screamed of pity and desire. She twisted her mouth from under his and buried her face in his jacket, her hands gripping the fabric as she shook with frustrated need.

"I'm young," she whispered after a minute. "I'll get over you."

"Will you?" His voice sounded odd. His big hands were in her hair, holding her head to him. They were just a little unsteady, and the chest under her forehead was shuddering with the force of his heartbeat.

"I'll have to," she said. She took a slow, soft breath. "It was enough that you and Justin have taken care of me all these years," she murmured. "I can't expect anything more from you. I shouldn't have. It was…just proximity, and a huge crush, and…and curiosity, that's all. I didn't mean—"

"Stop it," he said harshly. He pulled her closer, enfolding her in his big arms, holding her, rocking her. "My God, stop it. Am I laughing at you? Am I making fun of how you feel, or trying to shame you for it? I never should have said that to you at the feedlot that day about hating the way you looked at me. I didn't mean it. I wanted you so badly all I could think about was getting you out of the car before I lost my head." He laughed coldly. "And a hell of a lot of good it did. I lost it anyway, that morning in your room, and scared the hell out of you."

"I didn't understand what intimacy was until then," she confessed quietly.

"And the way I was holding you made you all too aware of what I wanted," he added with a faint laugh.

She flushed. "Yes."

He smoothed her hair, noticing the way her body was resting against his, so trustingly, even though he was just as aroused now as he had been the morning he'd mentioned. "And now it doesn't frighten you, does it?" he whispered, tilting her eyes up to his.

She searched his face softly. "No. Nothing about you frightens me or embarrasses me."

He touched her cheek, her mouth, and his powerful legs trembled at the contact with hers. "Not even knowing how badly I want you?"

She shook her head. "Not even that. I—" She dropped her gaze.

"You—" He made her look at him. "Say it," he whispered. "Say the words. I want it all."

She should have denied how she felt. Or run. Something. "I love you," she whispered with faint anguish in her tone.

His eyes caressed her face. "Such big eyes," he breathed. "So soft. So full of secrets." He bent and drew his mouth tenderly against hers. "You're very special to me, Abby. Part of my life. I wish I could give you what you want. I wish I could give you back those words and offer you a future. But that would cheat us both ultimately. Marriage should be a joint commitment, with a foundation of shared love." He sighed bitterly. "I…don't know how to love. Justin and I were raised by our father, Abby. Our mother died when I was born. We never had a woman's touch, and until your mother came along, Dad went from one woman to another like a bee to pollen." He toyed with a strand of her hair. "I don't understand commitment, because I never got a good look at it. The only thing I know about love is that it doesn't last. Look at Justin. See what happened to him because it all went wrong."

"At least he took the chance," she said gently. "And it does last. Or didn't you see how Justin and Shelby looked at each other while they were dancing?"

"Is that your idea of a perfect relationship?" he asked with a cold laugh. "A little love, followed by years of hating each other?"

"What's your idea of perfection, Calhoun?" she replied. "A succession of one-night stands and a lonely old age at the end of the road, with no family, no one to love you, nothing to leave behind?"

He scowled down at her. "At least I won't die of a broken heart," he said.

"No," she replied. "You won't." She pushed at his chest, but he wouldn't move. "Let me go, please."

"Why?"

"Because I've got a lot of work to get through."

"And a date with Tyler," he added mockingly.

She glanced up. "Tyler is solid, capable, very masculine and a good marriage risk. He isn't afraid of commitment. He'll make a good husband."

"You aren't marrying Tyler," he said shortly.

"Not unless he asks me," she agreed.

"You aren't marrying him even if he does."

"How do you plan to stop me?" she asked curiously.

"Guess."

She cocked her head, staring up at his stubborn face. "Why bother? You don't want me, except in bed. I want someone who can love me."

He shifted restlessly. "Maybe love can be taught," he said uncomfortably. He stared down at her hands on his chest. "Maybe you could teach me how."

She didn't feel as if her feet were touching the floor anymore. Could she possibly have heard him say that?

"I'm only twenty," she reminded him, "and your ward, and you don't want commitment—"

His mouth covered hers in midsentence, tenderly probing, pushing at it, savoring it. "Kiss me, Abby," he whispered into her mouth.

"I don't want—" she tried to protest.

"Love me, baby," he breathed.

Her arms slid under his jacket and around him. She pressed close, holding him, giving him her mouth with all the wonder and generosity of her love for him. She felt his lips smile against hers, heard his soft breathing, and then he increased the pressure of his mouth and his arms and she went under in a maze of stars.

A long time later, he groaned and his mouth slid to her throat, his arms contracting as he tried to breathe. "That," he whispered roughly, "was a mistake."

She could hardly get her own breath, and she knew it was much harder for him. She smoothed his cool, thick hair, gently soothing him, comforting him as he fought for control.

Her lips pressed light, undemanding kisses to his cheek, his temple, his closed eyelids. He stood very still, giving her that freedom with a sense of wonder at how it felt to be caressed so tenderly.

His eyes opened when she stopped. "That was a nice touch," he whispered, cupping her face in his warm hands. "Have you been talking to Misty again, or did you just think it might calm me down?"

"I read it in a book," she confessed, lowering her flushed face.

"Reading about it and doing it are pretty different, aren't they?" he asked gently.

"Yes." She was still trying to breathe properly. Her fingers toyed with a button on his patterned shirt. He was warm, and she loved the feel and smell and closeness of his body towering over her.

"I've never made love to a virgin," he whispered. His mouth touched her forehead with breathless tenderness. "I'd have to hurt you a little, maybe, at first."

She felt waves of embarrassment wash over her at the vivid pictures in her mind. His big, nude body over hers in bed, covering her, his hands holding her…

"Does it always hurt?" she asked shyly.

"Not for a man," he whispered, lifting his eyes to hers. "Not for you, either, if I could keep my head long enough to arouse you properly."

Her heart was going like a trip hammer. "H…how… would you?"

He kissed the very tip of her nose. "Go out with me and I'll show you."

"On a date?" she whispered.

"Mmm-hmm." He nuzzled his cheek against hers. "Tomorrow night. I'll take you to Houston. We'll wipe out the bad memory of that last time there. We'll dance and walk." He brushed his mouth over her ear. "Remember, I have an apartment there," he said slowly.

She closed her eyes. "No. I won't go to your apartment."

"It isn't the last century," he whispered. "We could be alone. We could make love."

Her face flamed. "No," she repeated.

"Abby…"

She pulled away from him, hating her own inhibitions and his attitude, as well. If he'd loved her, it might have been different. But he didn't. He wanted her. And after that first time, she'd be just like every other woman he'd slept with. She'd be just another one of Calhoun Ballenger's conquests, an ache that he'd satisfied and forgotten. A used toy.

"I have work to do," she said, and tried to smile. "And…I don't think I'll go to Houston with you, thanks all the same."

He realized only then what she thought. He'd made it sound as if he was going to round off the evening with a night in bed. He'd made it sound cheap, and that hadn't been his intention at all. He'd meant that he'd make love to her, very light love, and then he'd take her home. He hadn't meant—!

"Abby, no!" he burst out. "I didn't mean what you think!"

She opened the door. "I have to go." She went out, and he followed her, intent on having things out. But as he reached for her, Justin came in with two businessmen. Abby escaped into the bathroom, shaking, broken inside by hopelessness and rejection. Calhoun not only didn't love her. Now he didn't even respect her.

Chapter 9

Abby was grateful that business kept Calhoun occupied for the next two days. She could hardly bear the thought of seeing him when he knew so well how she felt about him. And now that he'd reduced their relationship to a strictly physical one, some of the joy had gone out of life for her. She hadn't expected that he'd actually proposition her. But if inviting her to his apartment wasn't a proposition, what was it?

She managed to avoid him when he was in the office that Thursday and Friday, since things stayed hectic. Abby was training a new secretary, and Calhoun seemed reluctant to discuss their private lives around the other woman. She was a year older than Abby, bright and quick-witted. And, unfortunately, already stuck on Calhoun. She had a habit of sighing and batting her long eyelashes every time he passed her desk. Abby was glad Friday was her last day. Having to watch Calhoun with a potential new conquest—the girl was blond and very pretty—was just unbearable.

There was a small farewell party for Abby late Friday afternoon. Justin and Mr. Ayker and the women who worked in the office had taken up a collection to buy her a beautiful cardigan in a pale yellow shade. There was a cake, too, and Justin made a brief speech about how valuable she'd been to them and how they hated losing her. Calhoun wasn't there. Abby left with mingled relief and disappointment. Apparently she wasn't even going to get to say goodbye to him. Well, that suited her. She didn't care if he was glad to be rid of her. Not one bit.

She cried all the way to Mrs. Simpson's house because she didn't care.

Tyler was right on time to take her to dinner. He looked good dressed up. He was wearing a navy blazer with tan slacks, a white shirt and a natty blue striped tie. He looked elegant and very masculine. His green eyes danced as Abby came downstairs in a gray crepe dress with a full skirt and a low, crosscut bodice with fabric buttons. Her hair was neatly styled, and she looked elegant and sexy.

"You look pretty," he commented with a slow smile.

She curtsied. "So do you. Good night, Mrs. Simpson," she called out. "I'll be in by midnight!"

Mrs. Simpson came to the doorway, grinning. "Mind that no good-looking woman tries to take Ty away from you," she teased.

"No chance of that," he replied carelessly, smiling down at Abby. "This dishy lady is enough for me. Good night, Mrs. Simpson."

"Good night," the older woman replied. "Have fun."

Tyler walked her out to his white Ford, opening the door for her. "I like your landlady. Her husband used to work for Dad. Did you know that?"

"She mentioned something about it," Abby told him. "She's a nice landlady."

He got in, started the car and pulled out onto the road. "Do you miss the big house?"

"I miss the brothers," she said quietly, fingering her small purse. "It's hard getting used to my own company. There was always something going on at home."

"Can I ask why you moved out?" he persisted, glancing in her direction.

She smiled at him. "No."

His eyebrows arched wickedly. "Don't tell me. Calhoun wrestled you down on the desk and tried to ravish you."

Her face turned scarlet. She cleared her throat. "Don't be absurd."

He chuckled. "It isn't absurd, considering the way he was watching you dance with me that night at the bar."

"He was too busy dancing with Shelby to notice," she murmured. "Justin went home and got drunk afterward," she added, neglecting to mention her own participation.

"Shelby cried all night." He sighed. "Hell of a thing, isn't it, Abby, the way they still care about each other. Six years, and they're as far apart now as they were then."

"And both of them dying inside," she added. She thought about herself and Calhoun and hoped that she wasn't going to end up like Shelby, grieving for a man she could never have. She forced a bright smile. "Where are we going?"

"To that new Greek restaurant," he told her. "They say the food is really good. Have you ever had Greek food?"

"No. I'm looking forward to trying it," she said, and the conversation was back on safe territory again and away from the disturbing subject of Calhoun.

Meanwhile, Calhoun was pacing in Justin's study at the house, his dark eyes black, his hands linked behind his back, scowling.

"Will you stop?" Justin muttered as he tried to add figures and ignore the distraction of his restless brother. "Abby's not our responsibility anymore. She's a grown woman."

"I can't help it. Tyler's been around. He's no boy."

"So long as Abby isn't interested in him, none of that will matter."

Calhoun stopped pacing and glared at him. "And what if she is? What if she's throwing herself at him on the rebound?"

Justin laid down his pencil. "Rebound from whom?" he asked, lighting a cigarette.

Calhoun rammed his hands into his pockets and stared out the dark window. "From me. She loves me," he said quietly.

"Yes," Justin replied, and for once his tone was sympathetic.

Calhoun hadn't realized how much Justin knew. He turned, his dark eyes curious, wary. "Did she tell you?"

Justin nodded. He took a draw from the cigarette, watching it instead of his brother. "She's young, but that could be an advantage. She isn't cynical or world-weary or promiscuous like most of your women. And she hasn't got a mercenary bone in her body."

"She'd want marriage," Calhoun replied tautly. "Happily ever after. I don't know if I could adjust to being married."

Justin looked up. "How are you going to take to a life without Abby in it?"

For an instant, Calhoun looked hunted. He stared at the carpet. "And what if it doesn't last?" he replied harshly. "What if it all falls apart?"

Justin blew out a cloud of smoke. "Love lasts. And if you're worried about being faithful to her," he added with a pointed stare, "you may find that fidelity isn't all that difficult."

Calhoun's dark eyes snapped. "Oh, sure. Look at you. Happily ever after. Your perfect relationship fell apart," he said, hurting and striking out because of it. "And how many women have you consoled yourself with in the past six years?"

Justin stared at him for a long moment, his eyes narrow and glittering. He smiled then, faintly. "None."

Calhoun didn't move. He hadn't expected that answer, despite Justin's clamlike attitude toward his private life.

"I had an old-fashioned idea that sex came after marriage with a woman like Shelby," Justin said quietly. "So I held back. After she broke it off, I found that I wasn't capable of wanting anyone else." He turned away, oblivious to Calhoun's shocked expression. "These days I find my consolation in work, Calhoun. I've never wanted anyone but Shelby since the day I met her. God help me, I still don't."

The younger man felt as if he'd been hit by a two-ton weight. His heart ran wild. Justin's words echoed in his mind. He couldn't even feel desire for the ravishing blonde Abby had seen him with in Houston. He hadn't felt it with anyone since that night he'd brought Abby home from the bar and seen her naked to the waist. Was that what he had to look forward to? Would he end up like Justin, imprisoned in desire for the one woman he couldn't have, alone for the rest of his life because he was incapable of wanting another woman?

"I didn't realize," Calhoun said quietly. "I'm sorry."

Justin shrugged. "One of those things," he said philosophically. He sat down behind his desk. "You may not believe in marriage, but you may find that a relationship can tie you up properly without a ring or a legal paper. And I'll throw your own question right back at you," he added, cocking his head at his brother. "How many women have you had since you noticed Abby?"

Calhoun's face grew hard and remote. He glared at Justin, then turned and left the room.

Justin lifted an eyebrow and chuckled softly to himself as he bent over his figures again.

Abby had a nice supper with Tyler, and the moussaka she sampled was delicious, like the elegant baklava they had for dessert and the faintly resinous wine they drank with their meal. But while she was listening to Ty talk about his new job, she was thinking about the empty future, about living without Calhoun. She'd gotten used to listening for his step in the hall late at night as he went to his room, to seeing him across the table, to watching television with him, to being near him at work. Life was so empty now, so cold. She felt as if she'd never know warmth again.

"The only bad part of it is that I'm going to get loaned out," Tyler was telling her resignedly as he drank a demitasse of Greek coffee after dessert. "Old man Regan has a daughter in Arizona who's coping with a dude ranch and two of her nephews for the summer. I'm going to be sent out there to get the place in shape, I gather, while my assistant looks after things here." He grimaced. "I hate dude ranches. And I don't much care for the woman trying to run this one. Apparently she thought she could and talked Regan into it, but she seems to be losing her shirt."

Abby glanced at him. "What's she like, do you know?"

"I don't have a clue. She's probably one of those feminists who think men should have the children and women should earn the living. I'll be damned if she'll tell me how to do my job."

Abby could see the fireworks already, and she smiled behind her cup at the mental image. Tyler was so much like Justin and Calhoun, a reactionary, a holdover from the old West. It would be fascinating to see how he coped with a modern woman.

He took her home minutes later, bending to kiss her cheek at the door of Mrs. Simpson's house. "Thanks for keeping me company," he grinned. "I enjoyed it."

"So did I." She smiled up at him. "You're a nice man. Someday you'll make some lucky girl a nice husband."

"Marriage is for—"

"The birds," she finished for him, sighing. "You and Calhoun ought to do an act together. You've got the chorus down pat."

"No man wants to get married," he told her. "Men get corralled."

"Oh, sure they do," she agreed. "By greedy, grasping, mercenary women."

"I'd marry you in a minute, Abby," he said. He was smiling, but he didn't sound as if he were joking. "So if Calhoun slips the noose, you just throw it my way. I won't even duck."

"You doll." She reached up and kissed his firm jaw. "I'll remember that. Good night, Ty."

"Good night. I'll give you a call next week, okay?"

"Okay."

She waved at him and then used her key and went inside. She climbed the stairs lazily, relaxed from the resinated wine and worn out from her long week of avoiding Calhoun. So it was a surprise to find the telephone ringing in her room, where she had her own private extension.

She put down her purse and sat on the bed to answer it. "Hello?"

A deep, familiar voice that made her pulse leap said, "Hello."

"Calhoun?" she asked softly.

"I can't sit up and wait for you anymore," he said. "So I thought I'd make sure you got home all right."

"I did."

"Where did you go?"

She lay back on the bed, her head on the pillow. "To the new Greek place."

"Ummm," he murmured, sounding as if he were stretched out on his own bed. "I've been there for business. dinners a time or two. Did you try the moussaka? It's delicious."

"Yes, that's what I had, and some of that resinated wine. It's very strong."

He paused. "Did you come straight home?"

She almost smiled at his concern. "Yes, I came straight home. He didn't even try to seduce me."

"I don't remember accusing him of it."

She touched the receiver gently. "Is everything all right at the house?"

"I guess so." There was a pause. "It's lonely."

"It's lonely here, too," she said.

Another pause. "I didn't mean what you thought I did," he said quietly. "I wouldn't take you to bed on a bet. You aren't the kind of woman to be used and thrown aside. I'm ashamed of you for thinking I could treat you like that after all these years."

Her heart ran away. She clutched the receiver closer to her ear. "But you said—"

"I said we could go to the apartment and be alone," he interrupted. "And that we could make love. I meant we could make a few memories and then I'd take you home." He sighed. "I'd probably do it bent double, but I never had any intention of taking advantage of the situation."

"Oh."

"So now that we've cleared that up, how about dinner tomorrow night?" he asked.

She hesitated. "Calhoun, wouldn't it be better if we just didn't see each other again?" she asked quietly, even though it broke her heart to say the words.

"I've looked out for you, watched over you and ordered your life for years," he replied. "Now you're grown, and things have happened between us that I never expected. We can't go back to the relationship we had, and we can't be intimate. But there has to be a way that we can keep each other," he said heavily. "Because I can't quite put you out of my life, Abby. I hate like hell going past your room at night and knowing you aren't in it. I hate watching television alone and sitting at a table alone when Justin has business dinners. I hate the feedlot because there's going to be another woman at your desk."

"She's blond," she reminded him.

"She isn't you," he said shortly. "Are you going to come with me or not?"

"I shouldn't...."

"But you will," he returned.

She sighed, smiling. "Yes."

"I'll pick you up at five."

"Five?"

"We're going to Houston, remember?" he laughed softly.

"Dining and dancing."

"Just that, if it's what you want," he said gently. "I won't even touch you unless you want it."

"That apartment," she asked hesitantly. "Have you... have you taken a lot of women there?"

He didn't answer her immediately. "While I was away those few days, I moved. I changed apartments," he said. "This one is across town from the one I had. And I've never taken a woman there."

She wondered at the switch, wondered why he'd bothered. Surely it couldn't be to protect her from the memory of his old life, in case one day she did go there with him?

"I see," she murmured.

"No, I don't think you do," he replied, his voice deep and soft. "Not yet, anyway. I'd better let you get to sleep. It's late."

She didn't want him to hang up. She searched for something to say, something to keep him on the line, but her mind was blank.

"You and Justin never came to blows over Shelby, I guess," she asked then, because it had just occurred to her that Justin had threatened to punch Calhoun the morning after the square dance.

"Justin and I had a long talk," he replied. "Not that I expect it to do any good. He's too set in his ways to bend, and he won't let Shelby get near him."

"Maybe someday he'll listen."

"Maybe." He sighed. "Five tomorrow. Don't forget."

As if she could! She touched the receiver as if she were touching him. "Good night."

"Good night, sweetheart," he said softly, and the line went dead.

She floated into her nightgown and into bed, hearing nothing but the endearment, that unexpected, beautiful word, until sleep finally claimed her.

It was the longest Saturday of Abby's life. She tried to sleep late, but she couldn't. She went downstairs and had breakfast with Mrs. Simpson and then she went back to her room and forced herself to watch television. Having Saturdays free was still new. At the feedlot, she'd always worked them. Now she had the whole weekend off, and she didn't know what to do with herself.

Time dragged all day long. She went for a ride just to give herself something to do and wound up in town shopping for a new dress to wear on her date with Calhoun.

She came out with a pretty red patterned silk skirt and matching sweater. It brought out her tan and made her look sophisticated. She thought about having her hair cut, but she'd gotten used to its length. She experimented with different hairstyles for an hour, only to brush it out and leave it around her shoulders afterward.

She was dressed and ready at 4:30. She tried to get

interested in a book while she waited. Those thirty minutes were going to be agony.

Apparently Calhoun felt the same way, because he showed up twenty minutes early.

She forced herself not to run to let him in, but she was breathless all the same as she looked up into his dark, quiet eyes.

"Hi," she said.

He smiled slowly, gazing approvingly not only at her outfit but at her hairdo, as well. "Hi," he replied lazily.

He was wearing a charcoal-gray suit with pale gray handtooled leather boots and a pearl Stetson. He looked so handsome that Abby could hardly believe he was really taking her out on a date. It was so new, so unreal.

"Are you sure you want to take me out?" she asked unexpectedly, her eyes troubled as they met his. "You don't feel sorry for me—?"

He put his thumb gently against her lips, silencing her. "I wouldn't take you to the post office out of pity," he replied. "Are you getting cold feet?" he added softly.

She grimaced and stared at his jacket. "Yes."

"I won't hurt you," he said, his voice quiet and deep. "I won't rush you or embarrass you."

She bit her lower lip. "It's just that it's…new."

"You'll get used to it." He moved restlessly. "Are you ready to go? I'm early, but I was afraid I'd get held up if I didn't leave while I could."

"Yes. I'll just get my purse."

She got her purse and her black velvet blazer, as well, and let him escort her out to the Jaguar. She got more nervous by the minute, which was absurd considering how long she'd dreamed of going anywhere with him. She could hardly talk, and her hands shook.

"How do you like living with Mrs. Simpson?" Calhoun asked on the way to Houston.

She smiled. "I like it very much." Her fingers toyed with the handle of her purse. "I miss the house sometimes. It's different, living alone."

He glanced at her, his eyes narrow. "Yes." He turned his eyes back to the road, frowning as he pulled a cigarette from the pack in his pocket and stuck it in his mouth. He reached for the car lighter, noticing her curious stare. "I'm nervous," he said without thinking, and then he laughed at his own confession. "That's one for the books, isn't it, Abby, with my reputation?"

She felt warm all over. She smiled, her eyes carefully lowered. "I'm nervous, too," she said.

"I'm not a virgin," he reminded her as he put the lighter against the cigarette.

"Rub it in," she sighed miserably.

"Don't make it sound like leprosy," he teased as he replaced the lighter in its hole beside the ashtray in the dash. "Frankly, I've had my fill of experienced women telling me what to do in bed."

She stared at him, torn between curiosity and jealousy. "Do women really do that?"

His eyebrows arched. He hadn't realized how innocent she really was. "Don't you go to movies?"

"I tried," she recalled. "You never would let me in to see the really good ones."

He whistled softly. "Well, well." His eyes brushed her slender body, then returned to the road. "You'll take a lot of teaching, won't you, tidbit?" he murmured.

She shifted against the seatbelt. "Which would probably bore you to death."

"I don't think so," he mused. "After all—" he lifted

the cigarette to his firm lips "—I could customize you."

She gaped at him. "Now I've heard everything!"

"Tell me you'd hate being my lover, Abby," he challenged softly, glancing her way.

She couldn't. But she couldn't quite admit the truth, either. She averted her face, burning with subdued irritation at his soft, predatory laughter.

They went to the same club where she'd seen him with the blonde, but this time was different. There seemed to be no barriers after the first few awkward minutes.

"I've never had rice made like this," Abby remarked as she enjoyed the small portion that came with her roast beef au jus.

"With scallions, you mean? It's unique. Like you," he added, and she looked up to find his eyes steady on her face. Intent. Unblinking.

She gazed back at him. He made her feel giddy when he looked at her that way. Her whole body tingled.

And she wasn't the only one affected. His heart was doing a tango in his chest at the way she was watching him, at her pleasure in his company. He even liked the way he felt himself, nervous and a little uncertain.

They finished their meal, and the dessert that followed it, in silence. As they lingered over a second cup of coffee, he finally spoke. "Want to dance?" he asked softly.

She swallowed. Her eyes traveled slowly over his big body, and just the thought of being pressed against him on the dance floor frightened her. She'd drown in pleasure, and he'd know it. He'd see how helpless she was, how vulnerable.

"I—don't know," she stammered finally, and swallowed the last spoonful of her apple pie.

"Are you really afraid to let me hold you in front of a roomful of people, Abby?" he asked with narrowed eyes.

She lifted her own gaze. "Yes."

"Why?" he persisted.

Well, why not be honest, she thought fatalistically. "Because I want you," she whispered softly, watching his expression become taut. "And because you'll be able to see how much."

Her lack of guile floored him. He couldn't remember a single woman in his past being quite so straightforward about such things. He took a slow breath and reached across the table for her hand, turning it over to trace the palm tenderly with a long forefinger.

"I want you just as badly," he said, watching her hand instead of her eyes. "And you'll be able to feel how much, as well as see it. And I still want to dance with you."

She was so hungry for him that her body was pulsing softly. Even having him know every thought in her mind, being vulnerable, didn't seem to matter anymore. She worshiped him with her eyes, and he looked up and caught her in the act.

"Let's stop pretending," he said quietly. "Come here."

He got up, drawing her with him. He led her to the small dance floor, where a band was playing a lazy tune, and when he pulled her close, she went without a murmur.

"Have you ever noticed how perfectly we fit together?" he asked against her hair as they moved to the music. His hand at her back contracted, bringing her even closer, and the sound of his voice at her ear was deliciously exciting. "I like the way you feel against me."

She could tell that, because his body was beginning to react in a totally masculine way to her softness. She stiffened a little, but the caressing motion of his fingers on hers relaxed her.

"It's all right," he whispered. "I won't hurt you."

"I know that." She closed her eyes, drowning in his nearness, in the music, in the magic.

He shuddered, a barely perceptible stiffening of his big body, and his hand pressed her against him for one wild second. "This is stupid," he said tautly.

"I tried to tell you that," she whispered shakily as her fingers contracted helplessly in his and she looked up into his eyes.

His jaw clenched. Everything she felt was in those worshipful eyes, in her face, in her body so soft against his. His mind whirled; he was floating. She wanted him.

"For God's sake," he groaned. "Let's get out of here."

Her gaze searched his hard, dark face, the eyes that blazed down into hers. He looked impossibly mature and experienced, and she knew she was out of her league. But she wanted to lie in his arms and let him love her. She wanted nothing in life more than to be alone with him now.

"I…" She swallowed. "I don't know how…I've never had to…about precautions, I mean…"

He bent, brushing his hard mouth against her soft one briefly, silencing her. "Are you scared?"

"Yes."

His nose nuzzled hers. "But you'd give yourself to me anyway."

She clenched her teeth. "Yes."

"And hate me afterward."

Her slender shoulders lifted and fell. "No."

Her expression touched him. "Do you love me that much?"

She lowered her eyes, but he tilted her chin up again and there was something new in his look, in his scrutiny of her face.

"Do you love me that much?" he whispered again.

Her eyes closed. "Yes!" she breathed.

His hand slid up her back into her long, thick hair and pulled her forehead against him, pressed it there as they moved to the rhythm of the music. "Precious," he said in a tone that could have burned water. She hardly heard him over the wild beating of her heart. His lips smoothed her forehead, brushing it tenderly.

"I won't make you pregnant," he whispered. "Come with me."

As if she had a choice, she thought shakily as she let him lead her off the dance floor. She'd never been so helpless in her life. All she could do was look at him with helpless need, love radiating from her oval face like fire from an open hearth.

He paid the bill and drew her out into the cold night air, tucked her in the car and drove across town without saying a single word.

Chapter 10

Calhoun had a penthouse apartment with a private elevator and a view of Houston that was breathtaking. It was furnished in tans and browns, with African carvings and weavings mingled with Western paintings and Indian rugs. It was an apartment that was welcoming despite its purely masculine ambience.

"Do you like it?" Calhoun asked, watching her from the closed door.

"Very much," she said, smiling. "It suits you."

He came into the room, his eyes never leaving her face. "How about something to drink? I can make coffee."

She shifted her eyebrows. "Coffee?"

His dark eyes narrowed. "Just because you got drunk with Justin doesn't mean you can expect the same courtesy here."

She shifted restlessly, her purse clutched against her waist. "Well, I didn't mean to get drunk with Justin."

"I'll bet the pair of you could hardly walk the next morning."

"We sort of leaned on each other," she confessed. She searched his hard face. "He was afraid you were going to use your experience to take Shelby away from him. He didn't come right out and say so, but it was implied."

"As if I could hurt him like that," he said curtly. His dark eyes wandered quietly over her face, tracing every soft line. "Did you care that I danced with her?"

She turned toward the window. "I like the scenery," she said, trying to change the subject, trying to breathe normally.

"Yes, I like it, too," he said finally. "I wanted something with a view of the city. And I have to spend a lot of time here on business, so that makes it a good investment."

She heard his steps coming closer, and she could feel his warmth at her back, smell the clean, spicy scent of him.

Her pulse jumped as his lean hands caught her waist and pulled her against his big body. She heard his breath and felt it in her hair as he wrapped her up in his arms from behind, rocking her lazily as they watched the city lights spread out below them.

He inhaled the floral scent of her body and the clean, shampooed softness of her hair all at the same time. He bent his head and brushed his mouth against her neck through her silky hair.

"I miss you," he said softly. "You haunt me."

"You'll get used to not having me around," she said sadly. "After all, up until five and a half years ago, you and Justin had the house all to yourselves."

"And then you moved in," he mused, linking his lean hands in front of her. "We got used to running feet and laughter, to music in the living room and movies on television and teenage girls in and out and hot-rodding young men speeding up the driveway."

"You were both very tolerant for old bachelors," she said. "Looking back, I guess I really cramped your style."

He stiffened a little, because it was true. She had at first. But now it hurt to look back, to remember his furtive affairs, his hidden amours. It hurt to think that there'd ever been a woman in his arms except Abby.

"A woman in the dark is just a body," he said softly. "And I never gave my heart, Abby."

"Do you have one?" she asked.

He turned her gently, putting her hand on his chest, over his white silk shirt, against hard, warm muscle and thick hair. "Feel it beat," he whispered.

"That isn't what I meant."

"I know." He looked down at her hand, feeling his body tauten at the light touch. He moved her fingers across his chest to a hard male nipple and held her palm there, letting her feel.

She glanced up at him, her blue-gray eyes wide and searching as he stroked her hand against the hardness.

"That happens to women," she whispered.

"And to men." He gently pulled her closer, his hands moving into her hair as he bent his head. "Unbutton my shirt. I'm going to show you how to touch me."

Her heartbeat sounded and felt unnaturally loud in the stillness of the room. But she didn't protest. Her fingers fumbled with the buttons, and eventually she had the shirt out of his slacks and away from his broad, bronzed chest with its thick covering of hair.

He smiled at her faint embarrassment. "Here. Like this." He pulled her hands against him in long, sensual strokes and watched their slender gracefulness as he drew them down to the wide belt around his slender hips. But when he tried to move them past it, she froze.

He searched her soft eyes quietly, sensing the turmoil in her heart. "You're very innocent," he said, his voice unusually deep and slow. "You've never touched a man intimately, have you?"

She traced a tiny pattern on his chest. "I've never done anything intimate with a man in my life, except with you."

He was incredibly pleased to hear that. His chin lifted. "I need more than a few chaste kisses," he said softly.

She flushed, staring at the heavy rise and fall of his chest. "I'm sorry."

He bent abruptly and lifted her, cradling her against him as he turned and walked down the hall with her.

He went through an open door, and she turned her head to find a huge king-size bed with a cream-and-chocolate quilted cover over it in a darkened room.

"Calhoun, no," she whispered, raising her eyes to his in the dimness of the heavily curtained room.

"I won't even undress you," he breathed, brushing her lips with his. "We're going to make a little love, and then I'll take you home. There won't be a risk. I give you my word on it."

"But you want me," she whispered in protest when he slid her onto the coverlet and stretched out beside her, his body so close that she could feel how aroused he was.

"Of course I want you," he said gently, smiling as he lay poised above her, his lean hands smoothing back her long, soft hair. "But there's no risk involved, as long as you don't do anything to knock me off balance."

She searched his dark face, loving every inch of it. "How could I do that?" she whispered.

"By doing anything I don't invite," he murmured deeply. "Don't touch me, or move against me, or kiss me unless I tell you how." He moved down then, drawing his open mouth lazily over her lips until he managed to get between them. "That's it," he whispered. "Just relax."

He was doing the most sensuous things to her mouth. It amazed her, the sensations he aroused so effortlessly. Her breath was already coming in gasps, and she felt her body tautening as what he did to her mouth began to affect the entire length of her.

"God, you're sweet to kiss," he whispered into her parted lips. "Come here, Abby."

He abruptly rolled over onto his back and turned her with him so that she was above him, looking down into his dark, dancing eyes.

"That's better," he murmured. "Do you feel less threatened on top?"

She colored faintly, and he laughed. Then he drew her mouth down over his and opened it, and the laughter stopped.

She felt his hands moving her, lifting her. She was beside him, then over him, and he had her hips, bringing them down completely over his.

"Don't do that," he whispered when he felt her tautness. "Just lie still and let me feel your body over mine."

She felt shaky. She trembled as his tongue began to probe gently around her lips and past them, teasing its way into the sweet darkness of her mouth.

She caught her breath, and he heard it. His dark eyes opened, looking up at her.

"They call it a soul kiss," he said softly. "It's intimate and wildly arousing and very, very suggestive. Let me kiss you that way."

She felt her legs tremble where they touched his. "You… you're already wildly aroused," she whispered unsteadily.

"I'm going to make you that way, too," he murmured. He turned her slowly so that she was on her back. His long, powerful leg insinuated itself between hers.

She stiffened as she felt his big, muscular body spread over hers, pushing her down into the mattress. His masculinity was blatant now. The intimacy was shocking, and the sensations it caused were a little frightening.

He saw her fear, and his hands slid into her hair, caressing as he let his weight down on her slender body, his elbows catching a little of it as he moved.

"I won't hurt you," he said softly. "Lie very still for me, Abby. I want to show you what passion is."

"I already know…oh!" She clenched her teeth. Her nails bit into the fine fabric of his jacket, and her eyes widened in shock when he moved against her. She felt him in a way that turned her face blood red with embarrassed knowledge, and a tiny cry forced its way out of her throat.

His mouth covered hers. His tongue teased, probed, withdrew, probed again and began a taunting invasion that was every bit as intimate as his huge, softly moving body on hers. She moaned. She grasped him. She bit at his firm, chiseled lower lip. Her tongue shyly encountered his and began to fence with it. She began to shudder, and so did he, and just when she was going under for the third time he slid away from her and gathered her against his side, holding her cheek to his shoulder while the trembling grew.

"Calhoun." Her voice broke.

"It's all right," he whispered. "I'll make it bearable."

His big hands found her jacket and eased it off. He unfastened the sweater where it buttoned over one shoulder, and levered it up lazily, unfastening the hooks of her lacy bra and tugging the whole of her upper covering over her head and moved it aside.

She started to cover herself, but his mouth was suddenly on her breasts, and what he did to them was too sweet, too addictive to protest.

She gave in, arching toward his mouth, drowning in his ardor. He knew exactly what to do, how to arouse her to a fever pitch. She let him, welcomed him, her body fluid in his hands, her voice softly inciting him.

He sat up for just a minute, long enough to strip off his jacket and shirt. Then he was poised over her, vibrantly male with his hair-roughened chest bare and muscular, his eyes glittering with desire as they caressed her own bareness.

"I can't stop you," she whispered shakily, tears stinging her eyes as she watched him come to her. "I don't want to stop you."

"I want to hold you like this," he whispered, levering his chest over her bare, aroused breasts, rubbing softly against her body. "Isn't it sweet, Abby? Skin against skin. Breast to breast in the darkness, mouth to aching mouth... Kiss me, sweetheart. Open your mouth and kiss me until you can't bear the wanting any longer."

She did. Her arms held him, trembling, her body welcomed the crush of his. The mattress moved under them and the air washed over her body while his mouth fed on hers, seduced hers, intimate and ardent and tender.

His mouth lifted seconds later, and he looked into her eyes in the faint light from the hall. "I don't think I can stop," he whispered, his voice oddly husky.

"I don't want you to stop," she moaned. "Oh, Calhoun, please, please...please!"

His mouth slid down to her breast, taking it inside. His hand went to the fastening of her skirt and loosened it. His lean fingers slid onto the soft skin of her belly, pressing there, savoring the soft skin.

"The...risk," she whispered shakily.

"Of a child?" he murmured against her breasts. He nuzzled her soft skin with his cheek, his eyes closed, the scent of her all around him, in his blood. His hand slid under her hips, lifting them hungrily into the hard contours of his own, holding her there with undisguised passion. "For the first time in my life, I'm not afraid of the consequences, Abby."

His mouth was over hers again, and she wasn't quite sure she'd heard him. Her mind was on fire, her body was burning. Her legs moved helplessly against his. She wanted him. She wanted all of him. She moaned as she tried to get closer, to absorb him, possess him. She felt savage and wild. She wanted to join with him, to be a part of the massive, muscular body that was slowly driving her mad.

Her arms reached up, her fingers tangled in his thick blond hair as she moved her hips sensually under his in movements that made him cry out.

"Abby—!" he bit off, shuddering.

"I love you," she sobbed.

His mouth was over hers, and he began to remove

her skirt with unsteady hands. It was going to happen. Here, now, she was going to know him in every way there was.

But in the middle of her feverish pleas, there was the sudden, unexpected pealing of the doorbell.

He paused, his body racked by shudders. "Oh, my God," he said, choking.

"Don't answer it," she whispered tearfully.

He lifted his head, pushing back sweaty hair. He was gasping for breath, his body vibrating with frustrated need, driving urgency. He shuddered. "I can't get up," he whispered with a hollow laugh. He pushed away from her and lay on his stomach, groaning, his lean hands speared into the pillow, crushing it.

Abby didn't know what to do. She knew better than to touch him. She lay there, not moving, sanity coming back slowly. She concentrated on trying to breathe while her heartbeat shook her.

The doorbell kept ringing. After a moment, Calhoun managed to sit up. He looked a little foggy as he got to his feet, but he was breathing almost normally.

"Are you all right?" she whispered shyly.

"I'm all right," he said softly. "Are you?"

At least he wasn't angry. "Yes," she replied, her tone equally soft.

He took a steadying breath and got to the door. Unexpectedly he switched on the light and turned to look at her, his eyes narrow, full of possession and something violent, dark, hungry.

Her breasts were mauve and peach, exquisitely formed, taut with arousal. Where he'd pulled her skirt down, he could see the graceful curve of her hips below her small waist.

"God, I could die looking at you," he said huskily. "I've never seen a woman so perfect."

She flushed, but the intensity of his delight in her was overwhelming. She sat up slowly, watching his gaze move to the firm thrust of her breasts, and she felt herself go hot with pride and pleasure.

He looked up then, catching the light in her eyes. "You belong to me now," he said. "As surely as if I hadn't stopped. We'll work out the details later, but there won't be anyone else for me from this night on. I'll never touch another woman until I die." And with that quiet, terse statement, he turned and left the room.

Abby wasn't sure she hadn't dreamed the whole thing. She got into her clothes in a daze, shaking with pent-up emotion. She wanted to cry and scream and laugh and dance.

He was talking to someone. His voice was curt and almost angry. Frowning, Abby stepped out into the hall, her mouth swollen, her hair in tangles, her silk skirt hopelessly wrinkled. As she went into the living room, she recognized Calhoun's guest. It was the blonde from the restaurant, the one he'd taken out the night Abby had gone to dinner with Justin.

"So that's why you didn't have time for me," the older woman said when she saw Abby. "My God, she's barely out of school!"

"Abby, go back into the bedroom," Calhoun said.

"Yes, Abby, go and hide," the blonde added viciously, although tears were visible in her big eyes.

But Abby didn't. She went quietly to Calhoun and slid her hand trustingly into his.

"I love him with all my heart," Abby told the other woman. "I guess you probably do, too, and I'm sorry. But I'd rather die than lose him."

The blonde looked at her for a long moment, and then at Calhoun. "It would have served you right if she hated you, as many hearts as you've broken," she cried, her lower lip trembling. "But that won't ever happen, any more than you'll ever love any one of us. Not even she can reach that stone you call a heart!" She turned to Abby. "You'll never have all of him." She laughed bitterly. "All he can give you is his body, and he'll soon get tired of yours and go off to conquer new worlds. Men like him don't settle down, honey, so if you're looking for happy endings, you'd better run like hell."

She gave Calhoun a final, bitter glance and was gone as quickly as she'd arrived.

Calhoun closed the door, his face hard, unyielding.

"I'm sorry you had to hear that," he said quietly.

"So am I." Abby searched his eyes sadly, wondering if the other woman was right about his lack of feeling. Perhaps she should run. But how could she, when she loved him?

His eyes narrowed as he saw the indecision and fear in hers. "You don't trust me, do you?" he asked. "You think she might be right, that you can't have a future with me."

"You said yourself that you didn't want to be tied," she replied. "I understand." She dropped her eyes. "Maybe I'm too young for marriage anyway. I've never been out on my own at all. I've hardly even dated. Maybe what I feel for you is just a crush and my first taste of desire."

She didn't really mean what she'd just told him, but it gave him an out if he wanted one. He'd wanted her in the bedroom, and perhaps he'd said things he didn't really mean. She didn't want him to feel obligated just because they'd almost gone too far.

But Calhoun didn't realize that she was trying to save him from himself. He took her words at face value and felt their impact as if they were bullets. She was telling him that she wasn't sure she loved him, and at the worst possible moment. When she'd put her slender hand so trustingly in his, he'd known for the first time what he felt for her. His feelings went deeper than lust, and they wouldn't fade. But now he was afraid to tell her, to put the emotion into words. She was admitting that she might have mistaken infatuation and desire for something lasting. She was young, all right, and inexperienced. He might be taking advantage of a natural step in her progression to womanhood. What if he risked his heart and she kicked it aside when she got through this phase? She was young, and she'd bounce back. But Calhoun had never loved before, and the thought of being rejected terrified him.

He stared down at her with bitter realization darkening his eyes to black. He'd fallen into the trap that he'd sworn he'd never be taken by. Now here they were, almost lovers, and she was telling him that it was all a mistake. He felt as if she'd hit him in the chest with an ax.

"Would you take me home, please?" she asked without looking at him.

He straightened. "Of course."

He turned toward the bedroom, and she sat on the sofa, reaching for the purse she'd tossed there when they'd first arrived. She sat twisting and turning it, listening to his quick, sharp movements in the bedroom while he dressed. Her eyes closed in mingled shame and embarrassment. It had only just occurred to her how many liberties she'd allowed him, how close they'd come to making love completely. She hadn't had the presence of mind to think of stopping, and neither had he. If that woman hadn't interrupted them—

Her face went hot. He'd been undressing her. He wouldn't have stopped at all, he hadn't had any intention of denying himself. And afterward, how would it have been? She'd have been eaten up by guilt and sorrow, and he'd have felt obligated to marry her because she'd been a virgin. He'd have been well and truly trapped.

She didn't take seriously anything Calhoun had said in the semidarkness of his bedroom, because men didn't think when they were engulfed by passion. Even though she was innocent, she knew that much. He'd wanted her for a long time, and tonight had been his one chance to get her into bed. He'd almost taken her. He knew she loved him, and it didn't even seem to bother him that he was taking advantage of something she couldn't help.

Calhoun came into the living room minutes later, pale and strained but neatly dressed. He'd even combed his thick blond hair. After one quick glance, she didn't look at him again. She stood up.

He opened the door for her, noticing her unnatural stiffness. "I don't know what to say, Abby," he said quietly. "I don't know how she traced me here."

"It doesn't matter," she replied, looking only as high as his chin. "It would be unrealistic to expect that we'd never run across any of your discarded lovers."

His dark eyes flashed fire. He reached beside her and slammed the door before she could get out, forcing her shocked eyes up to his angry ones.

"And that's what you think you would have been if she hadn't interrupted us?" he asked coldly.

She ground her teeth together to keep from breaking down. "You weren't going to stop," she said.

"I *couldn't* stop," he corrected. "Any more than you

could. If you want to know, it was a first. I've always been able to pull back before."

"Should I be flattered?" she asked on a trembling laugh. "Because I'm not. Bodies are cheap."

"Yours isn't," he returned. "Yours is young and sweet and exquisitely formed. Innocent, when I've never had innocence in my life. I might have been half out of my head, but I'd have managed to make you want me back and I wouldn't have hurt you."

"And after you were through?" she probed, lifting her pained eyes.

He touched her swollen lips with a cool forefinger. "That would have taken all night," he said softly. "And by then you wouldn't have had any doubts left about where we stood with each other. I'd have made sure of it."

She flushed. "I'd have been another conquest…."

He drew her against him, sighing heavily as he smoothed her long, dark hair and felt her body shake with soft sobs.

"It's just frustration, sweetheart," he whispered at the top of her head. "You wanted me and I wanted you, and neither of us had fulfillment, that's all. It passes."

Her curled fingers pressed against him while tears ran down her pale cheeks. "I hate you," she cried.

He only smiled, because he understood. He kissed her hair gently. She was so very young. Too young, probably. He drew in a slow, sad breath and wondered how he was going to live without her.

"You've got to see Maria about your birthday party," he said after a few minutes. "She's going to hire a caterer. And you'll have to provide a guest list for us. I can have one of the women at the office send out the invitations."

She drew back, sniffing, and he pulled out a handkerchief and mopped her face. "You don't have to do that," she mumbled.

"We want to." He touched the handkerchief to her red eyes. "I won't come near you until then, Abby," he added to her surprise. His dark gaze was quiet and unblinking, and it did wild things to her pulse. "I won't call you, or take you out, or see you until then."

"Because of tonight?" she asked with what dignity she still possessed.

"In a way." He put the handkerchief away and searched her face. "You're afraid of giving in to me, aren't you?"

She moved restlessly.

"Aren't you?" he persisted.

She bit her lower lip. "Yes."

"Why?"

"I won't have you forced into a marriage you don't want," she said warily. "Calhoun, you aren't a marrying man. You even told me so."

He brushed his mouth against hers, and he nuzzled her nose with his, teasing her lips, playing with her mouth.

"Abby, I told you not so long ago that my playboy days were over, and I meant it," he said softly. "I haven't lived like a recluse, but in the past few years, I've settled down. And if you want the truth," he added, resting his forehead on hers, "I haven't thought of any other woman since the night I found you bare-breasted on your bed, little one. You've been in my bed every night since then, a vision that haunts me from dawn to dusk."

Her heart jumped straight up. He'd never lied to her. He wasn't doing it now, she knew.

"Me?" she whispered.

He smiled gently. "You." He brushed her mouth lazily with his. "And if you'd given yourself to me in my bedroom a few minutes ago," he whispered, "we'd have been on our way to get a marriage license by morning."

"Because of your conscience?" she asked.

He chuckled softly. "Because of my body," he breathed. "Lovemaking is addictive. The way I want you, little Abby, I'd have you pregnant by the end of the first week."

She flushed wildly and hid her face from him, feeling his chest shake with laughter.

"Did you hear what I said," he whispered, "when you warned me about the risk?"

Her heart ran wild. "Yes."

His mouth bit at hers. "Didn't it seem an odd response for a philandering playboy to make?"

"You wanted me—"

"God, I still do!" he breathed. "But a man interested in nothing but a good time is sure as hell not interested in making babies, Abby."

"Stop that!" she whispered.

He smiled against her mouth, delighting in her innocence, in her reaction. He wasn't worried anymore. Now, at last, he knew why she'd said what she had in front of his visitor. She'd been offering him a way out. But he didn't want one. He wanted Abby. He wanted a future.

"I'll take you home now," he said gently. "And you can have until your birthday to think about me and miss me and want me. And then, if you can't stand it anymore, I'll give you a birthday present you'll never forget."

"What?" she asked breathlessly.

He covered her open mouth with his own. "Me," he breathed into it.

Chapter 11

Abby pondered that odd remark for the next few lonely weeks. What had Calhoun meant, that they were going to become lovers? Or had he meant something quite different?

He'd taken her home after that last, passionate kiss, and he hadn't made another single personal remark to her. He'd talked about the feedlot, about things at the house, even about the weather. And he'd left her at Mrs. Simpson's with a warm, secretive smile, contenting himself with a chaste but breathlessly tender kiss on her forehead.

As he'd promised, he hadn't called or come visiting. She hadn't seen him or heard from him since that night. It had been hard going, too. She'd stopped by Misty's a time or two, pretending to be happy so that her friend wouldn't ask too many questions. Tyler had asked Abby out again, but she'd refused without really understanding why. She wanted only the memory of Calhoun. If it was all she could ever have of him, it would be more than a lot of lonely women had.

She enjoyed her work at the insurance office, and her bosses were good to her. She settled in without any problem, but she went home to a lonely room, and as the days went by she was almost frantic with the need to see Calhoun.

She'd gone to the Ballenger house to talk to Maria about the party, and she'd left a list of guests for Justin, but to her disappointment both the brothers had been away at the time. She'd managed to get nothing out of Maria, either, except for a careless remark that everything was fine at home and the brothers seemed to be very happy. Which did nothing for Abby's self-esteem, especially since she missed Maria's wicked, conspiratorial smile.

The night of the party, Abby drove herself to the Ballenger house. She felt starved for the sight of Calhoun. All her memories and all her fantasies only made it worse.

She was wearing a long electric-blue gown that enhanced her blue-gray eyes and emphasized her exquisite figure. It had soft fabric straps and a crisscross bodice, a fitted waist and a long, narrow skirt. She wore her hair up in a braided coiffure with wispy little curls hanging beside her ears and curling on her forehead. She looked mature and sophisticated. She might not be beautiful, but she felt it tonight, and her face radiated with a glow that only the anticipation of seeing Calhoun could give her.

Maria opened the door and hugged her impulsively. "So lovely," the older woman sighed. "Everything has worked out so nicely, even the band was on time. Your guests have started arriving. The Jacobses are in the living room with Justin."

Abby winced, but Maria shook her head.

"No, it is all right," she said quickly. "Señor Justin and Señor Tyler have been talking cattle, and Señorita Shelby—" Maria smiled sadly. "Her soft eyes feed on Señor Justin like dry flowers welcoming rainfall. It breaks my heart."

"And mine," Abby said gently. "I'll go and keep her company."

She walked into the living room and smiled at Shelby, who was wearing a long green velvet skirt with a simple chemise top in white silk. She looked exquisitely lovely. Justin and Tyler, in dark suits, rose as she entered the room, both pairs of masculine eyes gazing appreciatively at her dress.

"Happy birthday, honey," Justin said gently, and went forward to brush his hard mouth against her cheek. "And at least a hundred more."

"I'll second that," Tyler grinned, his green eyes dancing as he bent and kissed her softly on the mouth. "You look delicious."

"Thank you both," she replied.

"I remember my own twenty-first birthday," Shelby sighed after she'd hugged Abby and congratulated her. "It was very special." Her eyes went helplessly to Justin, who stood very still and looked at her, his dark eyes full of emotion.

Abby could have cried. She hadn't understood before, but now she knew how devastating it could be to want someone that much. She looked around the room. There were several other people there, friends from school, who waved and lifted their glasses in her direction. She smiled back, but her heart was getting heavier by the second.

"Justin, where's Calhoun?" she asked finally.

Justin took a draw from his cigarette and dragged his gaze away from Shelby. Abby had asked the question he'd dreaded ever since she'd walked in the door. "I don't know if he's going to make it, honey," he hedged, because he didn't know where in hell Calhoun was either. She looked devastated, so he improvised. "He said to tell you happy birthday and—Abby!"

She couldn't help it. She burst into tears, shaking with the disappointment. "I'm sorry…" she sobbed.

"Shelby, take her into the study, please," Justin said.

"Of course." Shelby put a gentle arm around her. "Abby, please don't cry. I know Calhoun would have been here if he could have."

"I'll be all right in a minute," Abby told Justin as they passed him and a quietly curious Tyler. "I'm sorry. It's been a long week," she added with a faint smile.

"I'll knock him through a wall for this," Justin said coldly. "I swear to God I will."

"No, you won't," Abby sniffed. "As Shelby said, I'm sure he had a good reason." She laughed coldly. "Probably a blond one…" Tears fell hotly again, and Shelby quickly got her out of the room, across the hall and into the study.

"Now sit down." Shelby helped her to the burgundy leather sofa. "I'll get you a brandy. Is that all right?"

"I hate him," Abby said, burying her face in her hands. "I hate him so much!"

"Yes, I know." Shelby smiled wryly and poured brandy into a snifter. She gave the glass to Abby, and watched her take a sip and grimace at the harsh taste.

Her blue-gray eyes lifted to Shelby's green ones. "I haven't even seen him in weeks," she said brokenly. "He hasn't called or come to see me. I didn't know why then, but now I do. He was letting me down easy. He knows how I feel, and he doesn't want to hurt me...."

"If it means anything, I know how you feel, too," Shelby said gently, her eyes soft and sad.

"Yes, I'm sure you do." Abby touched the older woman's hand. "Justin never looks at anyone else. Calhoun said once that he supposed Justin would die loving you."

"And hating me, all at once," Shelby sighed. "Justin thinks I slept with someone else. He believed my father and a crony of his, and I've never been able to make him listen. As if I could have let any other man touch me, ever!"

Abby stared at her, momentarily distracted. "Oh, Shelby," she whispered.

Shelby grimaced. "Stubborn, proud, hardheaded man." Her eyes lifted. "I'd die for him."

"I hope it works out someday."

The older woman sighed. "Miracles still happen occasionally." She searched Abby's eyes. "Will you be all right now?"

Abby finished the brandy. "Of course I will. I don't care if Calhoun misses my party. I can have a perfectly good time without him. After all, I was only his ward and now I'm not anymore. He's just another man." She got up, smoothing her hair. "I'd better fix my makeup."

She went to the mirror and repaired her lipstick and powder, but there was very little she could do about her red eyes. Then she followed Shelby out the door.

The band was good. They played a succession of dreamy waltzes and country-and-western songs, which

their lead singer belted out in a smooth baritone. Abby
danced every dance, some with Justin, some with Tyler,
and a lot with old school friends. But still Calhoun didn't
make an appearance. Abby grew more vivacious by the
minute to cover up her misery.

She was dancing much too close to Tyler in a lazy
two-step, when she felt eyes on her back. Without
looking, she knew Calhoun had arrived. He'd spoiled
her party by not showing up until it was almost over,
and she hated him. Having settled that in her mind, she
kept her eyes closed and kept dancing.

"Calhoun's here," Tyler murmured into her hair.

"So what?" she said icily.

His eyebrows arched. He glanced at Calhoun, who
was thunderously angry, and then at Justin, who was
heading toward his younger brother with an expression
that would have made a lesser man than Calhoun back
off.

"Abby, Justin's going toward Calhoun with blood in
his eye."

"Good," she muttered. "I hope he kills him."

"Abby!"

She bit her lower lip. "I don't care."

"You don't care like hell," Tyler replied curtly. He
stopped dancing and held her by the arms. "Stop it. If
you want him, for God's sake, show him that you do.
Don't pout and hem and haw until you lose him."

"You don't understand," she began.

"Abby, look at Shelby and Justin," he said quietly. "Is
that how you want to end up?'

She searched Tyler's face and then looked over to
the doorway, where Justin and Calhoun were talking
in terse monosyllables. "All right," she said wearily.

He smiled. "Good girl. Go on."

She hesitated, but then she walked away. Tyler watched her go, a faint sadness in his own eyes. That was quickly erased when Misty Davies wandered over in a frothy gold party dress and asked him to dance.

Justin stopped talking when Abby came near. He glared at Calhoun. "Tell it to Abby," he said shortly. "She's been having a hell of a good time, though, all by herself."

Justin smiled faintly at them and wandered off to talk to another of the guests, leaving a cold-eyed Calhoun and a fuming Abby staring at one another.

"Thank you for coming," she said with faint hauteur. "I'm having a lovely time."

"How could you think I'd willingly treat you like that?" he asked quietly. "Turn my back on you, deliberately arrive late, embarrass you with your guests… Oh, God, don't you know me better than that?"

He disconcerted her. She looked up at him helplessly. "What happened?"

"I ran the Jaguar into a ditch and damned near wrecked it," he said with a mocking smile. "I was going too fast, and I took a curve where there'd been an oil spill that I didn't know about."

Her face went white. She saw a graphic mental picture of him lying in a ditch, dead. It erased all her stupid suspicions and left her shaking.

Without a word, she pressed hard against him. She held him, trembling, oblivious to her surroundings, to everything but Calhoun.

"You're trembling," he said, faintly surprised. His big hands went to her back, where it was bare over the deep plunge of her dress. "I'm all right, honey."

She held him tighter, fighting tears. The trembling grew worse, and she couldn't seem to stop.

"For God's sake…!"

He drew her out of the room, one big arm supporting her, and into the study. He locked the door behind them, shutting out the music and muffled conversation and other party sounds. His dark eyes looked down into her wild, pale ones.

"I wouldn't have missed your party on purpose, little one," he said gently.

That was the old Calhoun, she thought wildly. Her guardian. Her protector. The kind, caring older man who looked after her and kept her safe. But he didn't look or sound like a lover, and she supposed that he'd used those weeks to good advantage, getting her out of his system. She felt sick and shaken, and she wanted nothing more than to go home and cry herself to sleep.

"No, I'm…I'm sure you wouldn't have," she said, her voice husky. She forced a smile. "It was kind of you and Justin to let me have the party here."

His dark eyes narrowed. He leaned back against the door, elegant in his evening clothes, the white silk of his shirt emphasizing his high cheekbones, his blond hair and dark skin, his powerful build. "You sound strange," he said. "You look strange."

"I've had a long week, that's all." She was beginning to sound like a broken record. "I'm enjoying my new job. I like it very much. We stay busy. And—"

"Stop it," he said softly.

Her eyes closed, tears burning them. Her hands at her sides tautened into fists and she fought for control. "I'm sorry."

"Come here, Abby," he said in a tone that she

remembered, deep with tenderness, soft with sensuality.

She opened her eyes. "I don't want pity," she whispered.

His chin lifted. "What do you want?"

She lowered her gaze to his highly polished shoes. "The moon," she said wearily.

He moved forward abruptly. One big, lean hand caught hers and pried it open. He placed something in it and curled her fingers around it. She frowned. Something small and thin and metallic…

She opened her hand. It was a ring, a very simple circle of gold without any flourishes or frills. It was a wedding ring.

He bent, lifting her. He carried her to the burgundy sofa and put her down on it. Then he knelt on the carpet beside her, his lean hands on her waist, his blond hair gleaming like the golden ring in the soft light from the ceiling.

"I love you," he said softly, holding her gaze as he said it.

Her eyes searched his, getting lost in their dark, unblinking intensity. "W-what?"

"I love you," he repeated. "I didn't know it until the night I almost made love to you, and even then I wasn't sure that I could settle down." He laughed faintly, watching her with eyes that adored her. "But I'm sure now. These past few weeks have been the purest hell I've ever known. A dozen times I've almost stormed over to your apartment at three in the morning to get into bed with you. I've thought about kidnapping you from work and carrying you off into the mountains. But I promised to give you time, and I have. Now I've run out of it. If you don't marry me, so help me, I'll ravish you where you sit."

"I'll marry you," she whispered. "But—"

"But what?" he whispered back.

Her lips parted as she let her shoulders droop, so that the silky fabric of her dress fell and revealed all of her breasts except the hard tips. "But wouldn't you ravish me anyway?"

His breath caught. "As if I needed asking…"

His hands finished the job, stripping the fabric to her waist. He sat looking at the soft, pretty swell of her breasts, watching her breathe for a long moment before he drew her toward him and bent his head.

She began to tremble when she felt his mouth on her soft, heated skin. Her hands cradled his head and she wept softly, kissing his hair, whispering to him. "I love you," she murmured. "I'm sorry I…made a fuss. I thought you were out with some woman, that you didn't want me…. Oh, Calhoun!"

His mouth had opened, taking almost all of one perfect breast inside to taste, to caress with his tongue. His lean hand was at her back, searching for a zipper, and in the next instant she was on the carpet under him, her body bare from the neck down except for her briefs and her stockings.

"I was in Houston buying a ring. Buying two rings. Your engagement ring had to be sized. It's a yellow diamond." He kissed her hungrily. "I got caught in traffic, and since I knew I was going to be late, I rushed back…too fast. But it's all right now, isn't it, sweetheart?" He eased his hands down her body, feeling her tremble. "Abby, suppose we make love right here?" he murmured, stroking her gently with his warm, hard fingers.

"Someone might come in," she whispered breathlessly.

He smiled as he bent. "I locked the door," he breathed into her open mouth. "I'm hungry."

"I'm hungry, too."

His nose nuzzled hers. "Or we could go up to my bedroom," he murmured huskily. "And lock the door. Even Justin wouldn't disturb us there."

"The guests…"

"They'll never miss us. They're too busy enjoying themselves. I want you, Abby. I want you for the rest of my life, until I die. And if I get you pregnant…" He lifted his head, searching her warm, soft eyes. "Would you mind having my child?"

She touched his mouth with aching tenderness. "I love you," she said. "I want to have lots of babies with you."

He actually shuddered. "You're very young."

She smiled. "All the better." She traced his heavy eyebrows with her finger. "I can play with them."

He smoothed back her hair, his eyes full of wonder. "Abby…I never dreamed how sweet it would be to belong to someone. To have someone of my own. And a family." He touched her breasts tenderly. "Ever since the first time I touched you, I've felt as if there'd never been a woman for me. You make it all new and exciting. You make me feel whole."

"You make me feel the same way." She reached up to find his mouth with hers, kissing him slowly, tenderly. "Justin won't like it if we go upstairs together."

"He won't see us," he whispered and smiled wickedly. "Where's your sense of adventure?"

"I'm nervous—"

"We'll be married by tomorrow afternoon. I've

already got the license. All we need is a blood test, and
we can have that in the morning.

"You rake," she said accusingly.

"Reformed rake."

"All right," she breathed.

He searched her eyes quietly. "I need you badly. But
I can wait if you want me to."

"You don't want to," she said.

He smiled. "I've felt married to you since that night in
my apartment, Abby. A piece of paper and a few solemn
words aren't going to tie me to you any more firmly
than I am right now. I love you, honey," he said softly.
"That's the beginning and the end of my life, wrapped
up in those words."

She pressed against him. "I love you so."

He helped her into her dress and led her out the back
door, around through the guest bedroom and to the rear
staircase. Then he picked her up, laughing softly, and
carried her upstairs. He'd just made it to the landing and
was turning the corner toward his own room when they
ran headfirst into Justin and almost went down on the
floor with the impact.

Abby gasped. Calhoun actually turned blood red.
Justin's eyebrows went up expressively. Then they just
stared at each other.

"Tired of dancing?" Justin asked after a minute, his
lips pursed mischievously.

Calhoun cleared his throat. "We were going to…"

"…talk," Abby improvised.

Justin's dark eyes went over Abby's face, reading all
the telltale signs there. Then he glanced toward Calhoun
and stared him down.

"Oh, what the hell," Calhoun muttered darkly. "You
know damned good and well where we were going and

why. But there's something you don't know. I love Abby. We're getting married tomorrow. The license is in my pocket."

"And the ring," Abby added, faintly embarrassed at being caught in such a compromising situation.

"Congratulations," Justin said pleasantly. "I couldn't be happier for both of you. And if I might just add, it's about time."

Calhoun shifted Abby. "Thank you."

"You'll be a lovely brother-in-law," Abby agreed.

"The very best," Calhoun added.

Justin smiled. "It won't work. I'm not going anywhere, and neither are you."

"Damn it, Justin!" Calhoun ground out.

"Twenty-four hours is just overnight," Justin continued. "Then you can both go to Houston and have a honeymoon in that penthouse apartment you bought."

"Listen here…" Calhoun began.

"Abby, you tell him how you really feel about this," Justin said, staring at her.

She grimaced, her hands linked around Calhoun's neck. She sighed. "Well, I love him," she said finally.

"I thought you wanted to," Calhoun said softly, searching her embarrassed face. "I'd never have forced you."

"Oh, I know that," she said, her eyes worshipful. "But I couldn't refuse you."

He smiled ruefully. "You're one of a kind," he said gently. "And I love you."

"I love you, too," she whispered, smiling.

He kissed her softly. "I guess we'd better wait, since Justin is going to stand there until he takes root."

"I guess we had," Abby murmured.

Calhoun put Abby on her feet. "Well, let's go

downstairs and dance, Abby," he said. "Then we can sing that terrific drinking song that Justin taught you."

Justin glared at him, looking uncomfortable. "You started that."

Calhoun's eyebrows lanced upward. "All I did was dance with Shelby."

Justin stared at him coldly. "And if you hadn't been my brother, I'd have broken your jaw for it."

There was a faint sound behind them, and Justin turned to find Shelby standing two steps behind him.

"Go ahead, Shelby, get an earful," Justin said icily. "Does it please you that after six years I still feel murderous when another man touches you?"

"That works both ways, Justin," Shelby said quietly. "Or didn't you know that it would kill me to see you with another woman?"

She turned and stormed off downstairs. Justin stared after her, shocked.

"Why don't you carry her upstairs?" Calhoun asked his brother with pursed lips. "Then Abby and I could stand on the landing and block your way."

Justin said something in Spanish that Abby was glad she didn't understand and stomped off downstairs.

Calhoun glanced at Abby's questioning face and grinned. "I'll tell you after we're married," he whispered in her ear.

And he did tell her two days later as they lay together in the big soft bed at his penthouse, sated and close in each other's arms as the sun drifted lazily through the blinds.

"What did Justin say to you the night you started to carry me upstairs?" she asked drowsily.

"He said that if he ever took Shelby to bed it would be

on a desert island with mines on the beach." he chuckled. "Poor Justin," he added quietly. "To love like that and not even have a memory to live on."

She lifted her eyes to his, her hand lazily stroking his thick, hair-matted chest. "What do you mean?"

"Justin never slept with Shelby," Calhoun said softly. "And since the engagement broke off, he's never slept with anyone else."

She caught her breath.

"It isn't so incredible, Abby," he mused, rolling over to look down into her soft eyes. The covers had long since been thrown off, and his dark gaze slid over her nudity with possession and exquisite memories of the night before. "I couldn't touch anyone else after I kissed you."

"That's very profound," she whispered, trembling as his lean hand stroked gently over her taut breasts and down over her belly to the silken softness of her thighs.

"It's that," he agreed, bending to brush his lips across her mouth. "Have I hurt you too badly, or is it all right if we make love again?"

She flushed, remembering their first time, the softness of his voice whispering to her to lie still after he'd realized how difficult it was going to be. And then he'd bridled his own needs so that he could rouse her all over again. The pain had been minimal, because the savage hunger he'd kindled in her had surpassed pain or fear or even thought. She'd given everything he'd asked in the end, her body so completely his that he could have done anything to her.

"I'm all right now," she whispered, adoring his hard face with her eyes. "You made it all right."

"You were very much a virgin, Mrs. Ballenger," he

said with faint traces of satisfied delight. "And it wasn't the easiest initiation."

She traced his chin. "I love you. And any way you loved me would have been all right."

He kissed her softly. "You make me feel humble."

"You make me feel wild," she gasped, arching as his hand moved. Her eyes widened as it moved again. "Yes…do… that…"

He smiled through his own excitement as she responded to him. He enjoyed her innocence as he'd never imagined he could. He held back this time, drawing out his possession until she was crying with her arousal, until she was almost in torment from the need. And then he eased down, tenderly, coaxing her to bank down her own fires and settle into a new and achingly sweet rhythm that brought with it a fulfillment beyond her wildest dreams, beyond even his experience.

Afterward, he cradled her against his hard, damp body, trembling as he held her, stroked her. She'd gone with him every step of the way, and she was exhausted. So was he. She made an adventure of lovemaking, an exquisite expression of shared love. It was something he'd never known in a woman's arms. Whispering softly, he told her that.

She smiled as she lay nestled against him. "I don't have anyone to compare you with," she whispered. "But on a scale of ten, I'd give you a twenty."

Calhoun laughed softly, closing his eyes and sighing contentedly as he felt her snuggle close to him, her body fitting perfectly against his.

"Abby, how would you feel about living in the old Dempsey place?" he asked unexpectedly.

She opened her eyes. "That big Victorian house that you and Justin bought last year? It's been remodeled and furnished, hasn't it? I thought you were going to use it for offices."

"I'd thought about it," he told her. "But I want to live there with you."

"There, and not with Justin?" she asked softly.

He touched her hair. "It will make life hell for him if we're under the same roof."

"Yes, I know. To see how happy we are will only point out what he's lost." She smiled. "I'll live with you wherever you say."

He searched her eyes gently. Then he folded her up against him and drew the sheet over their damp bodies. "I love you, Abby," he said drowsily.

"I love you, too." She slid her arm across his broad chest and sighed contentedly. It was spring, and soon the pastures would be dotted with wildflowers and seed would begin sprouting everywhere. She closed her eyes, thinking about the long horizons and lazy summers and the promise of children playing around her skirts while she sat in the circle of Calhoun's arm and watched the cattle graze. It sounded like the most exciting kind of future to share—with a long, tall Texan at her side.

* * * * *

THE
Essential
COLLECTION

by Diana Palmer

YES! Please send me *The Essential Collection* by Diana Palmer. This collection will begin with 3 FREE BOOKS and 2 FREE GIFTS in my very first shipment—and more valuable free gifts will follow! My books will arrive in 8 monthly shipments until I have the entire 51-book *Essential Collection* by Diana Palmer. I will receive 2 free books in each shipment and I will pay just $4.49 U.S./$5.39 CDN for each of the other 4 books in each shipment, plus $2.99 for shipping and handling.* If I decide to keep the entire collection, I'll only have paid for 32 books because 19 books are free. I understand that accepting the 3 free books and gifts places me under no obligation to buy anything. I can always return a shipment and cancel at any time. My free books and gifts are mine to keep no matter what I decide.

279 HDK 9860 479 HDK 9860

Name	(PLEASE PRINT)	
Address		Apt. #
City	State/Prov.	Zip/Postal Code

Signature (if under 18, a parent or guardian must sign)

Mail to the **Reader Service:**

IN U.S.A.: P.O. Box 1867, Buffalo, NY 14240-1867
IN CANADA: P.O. Box 609, Fort Erie, Ontario L2A 5X3

ECDPBPA11